PIKE

THE PAWN DUET, BOOK ONE

TM FRAZIER

Born into chaos. Baptized in the gutter.

I was raised by the violent laws of the streets, spilling blood without the hindrance of useless emotions or connections.

Unfeeling. Unloved. Alone.

My life was perfect.

Until her.

While on a manhunt for a mysterious enemy, one hell bent on taking both my business and my life, I find Mickey. She's covered in mud, rambling nonsense, and clearly out of her mind.

She's also a distraction I don't need.

That is until I discover a connection between the girl and my enemy.

Mickey isn't a distraction anymore.

She's the perfect weapon.

One I'll use to exact my revenge.

The plan is an easy one, but there's something about Mickey that's making it more and more difficult.

A familiarity I can't place. A need I can't explain. A want I have to deny.

After all, she's not mine to keep.
She's mine to sacrifice.

For the two people who are my entire world.
My sun and my moon.
My always and my forever.
L&C

"From the deepest desires often come the deadliest hate."

SOCRATES

PROLOGUE

PIKE

LOVE IS A PLAGUE, INFECTING THE MASSES WITH THE LIE OF *HAPPILY ever after.*

It's the ultimate religion, followed by those who have faith that it will save their wretched souls and give them some sort of deeper purpose. That love is what makes life worth living.

Bullshit.

Love is a fucking cult. A stampede of hopeful morons all rushing to jump off the same cliff that has claimed the lives of millions before them. Through the fog, they're unable to see their fate, what love really has waiting for them at the bottom.

Nothing but a gruesome tangle of carnage.

So, they jump.

And when all is said and done, love doesn't lead them to find purpose or hope or meaning in this life.

It ends with joining the fucking pile.

Another notch carved on the handle of love's gun.

The only true end to the plague is death or something that feels a lot like it when the infection spreads to the heart and soul, crushing a man from the inside.

Love is messy, bloody, and ignorant.

1

Hatred is born in the absence of love's false promises. An evolution of man.

Hate is easy. Pure in its simplicity.

It doesn't disappoint or lead astray.

There are no false promises, no fog clouding what's waiting at the bottom of the cliff.

Hate is a product of where I came from and a direction to where I'm going.

Logan's Beach.

It's a town made up of equal parts sand and sadists.

Beach and blood.

Saltwater and sins.

Canals and chaos.

The overgrown, empty fields house the perfect soil in which the seeds of hatred are planted and flourish, producing an army of soulless men. The blood in their veins, replaced by the flowing green of greed. They wield weapons instead of hands, and stones instead of hearts. Encroach on their paths, and you will be cut down.

The only law in this town is power. And the lengths you're willing to go to obtain that power can be both astonishing and horrifying. Respect is earned through bloody acts of violence and the kind of brutality that outside of this town only exists in nightmares.

My power lies in my truth. I have no false notions about who I am or what I'm capable of. I don't fear retaliation, retribution, or the fucking reaper himself.

I approach life without my weapon hidden behind my back but in my hands and in your face because my seed wasn't planted at birth, but rather by circumstance.

I'm not a victim. I'm simply the result. A product of Logan's Beach.

An outcast. An outlaw. Out for fucking blood.

I'm prepared for anything and anyone.

Except *her*.

My life after Mickey is a live grenade being tossed into the air like a child's plaything.

While I'm distracted, trying to keep everything I've worked for from exploding, she somehow manages to slip her small feminine fingers past all of my barriers, reaches into my black fucking soul…

And pulls the fucking pin.

CHAPTER ONE
MICKEY

FOUR YEARS AGO

MAMA AND PAPA ALWAYS BEAM WITH PRIDE WHEN THEY TELL people I have a photographic memory, even though I feel like the accomplishment is the least spectacular among those of my three younger sisters. Mallory, thirteen, is already on the junior Olympic swim team. Maya, sixteen, recently received her early acceptance letter to Stanford. Mindy, seventeen, paints spectacular watercolor landscapes and landed her first solo gallery show in Miami next month.

Then, there's me. Mickey, nineteen, photographic memory, high IQ, socially inept.

Eh, seems pale by comparison. Maybe, because I've watched them work so hard to reach their goals while my accomplishments are merely products of something I was born with. I never had to try to be smart or remember things.

I just am. I just can.

I hear Papa's voice in my head from dinner last month with my aunt and uncle. *"Bob, did I ever tell you that Mickey here has a photographic memory? It's astounding. She can remember every detail of everything she sees. Never seen anything like it. Bob, give me your driver's license. She'll remember the numbers in two-seconds flat."*

I chuckle to myself at the image of Bob's astonished face when I did just that, taking a quick glance at his drivers' license before handing it back and reciting not just his license number, but his birthday, the date he got his license renewed, and the fact that he's an organ donor. I added the part about him having a ketchup stain on his collar in the picture for good measure.

My memory has always been my superpower. It's never failed me.

My smile falls.

Until today.

Today, Papa's brag is a lie.

Because something happened today, and for the first time in my life, I can't remember what.

The memory is there, but it's sitting inside my brain like a shredded picture, floating in the wind. Just when I feel like I'm getting close to it, it's gone again. It's like catching something moving in the corner of your eye only to turn around and realize that nothing's there.

It's as if I'm chasing ghosts.

The sound of my sisters' laughter brings me back to the present. I brush off the uneasy feeling and plaster a bright smile on my face.

Whatever happened must not have been that important. Because if it was, I'm sure I'd remember. Because it's who I am. I'm the daughter who remembers.

Whatever is going on with my memory is going to have to wait because I refuse to let anything bother me, especially not here, my happy place.

My family and I vacation here in Logan's Beach every summer. We have a small timeshare right on the beach. All of my greatest memories took place in this town. I lost my first tooth here. I had my first almost-kiss on the pier, pulling away at the last second after spotting whatever gross thing was stuck in Hudson Yontz's braces, but the memory still makes me smile. My mom taught me how to swim in the pool of the time-share here. My sisters and I even won a fishing tournament here. We called our team the Snook Sisters and that year, the Snook Sisters took home first place. You would have thought we'd won the lottery instead of a forty-five-dollar gift certificate to Master Bait & Tackle.

The warmth of the sun begins to cool, and the unrelenting heat fades from the back of my neck leaving a cool spot in its place as the breeze brushes across my wet skin.

I glance up to the sky and notice the sun dropping into the horizon.

Sunset already? Where did the time go? Didn't we just leave the timeshare to go kayaking a few minutes ago?

We did. That, I remember. We packed up the van. Strapped the kayaks to the roof. Stopped to buy more sunscreen.

Didn't we? Or was that last year?

Was it raining? I think I remember rain.

It's all blurry.

I mean, time always flies by during our summers here. It's not that unusual for me to lose track of it.

But not of your memory.

It's fine. It will all be fine. I refuse to enter into that line of conversation again with my inner voice. After all, there's only so much time left. It's our last summer here as a family, and I want to enjoy every minute of it.

The sign that says *Welcome to Logan's Beach* glows green under the fading light as I approach. Every week during the summer, there's either a large black spray-painted phallus across the lettering or a patch of paint covering said phallus.

Today, it's a paint patch.

I smile to myself as I slowly walk past the sign. My feet ache from walking. Always the drama queen, I hear Mallory complaining about hers behind me, and I roll my eyes.

Mom assures her we are almost there. I reply with a sarcastic "Are we there yet?"

Nobody laughs but Papa.

I listen on as Papa tells a bad knock-knock joke that makes my sisters and my mom simultaneously groan. Papa's weird like me. Not only do we share the same high IQ, but also the same cheesy sense of humor. I'm the only one who laughs at his joke, and I'm rewarded with one of his famous winks.

Mindy chides me for encouraging him and groans even louder when he starts telling another joke.

Tormenting my sisters is even somehow sweeter here.

Even sharing a bathroom with my three sisters is more tolerable here than it is at home, and the one at home has two sinks where the one in the timeshare only has one.

As we walk, I'm leaving a snail-like trail of water on the pavement behind me. My clothes have gone from wet to damp under the heat of the sun. My jean shorts chafe at the inside of my thighs, rubbing the skin raw with each step. My wild mass of hair is a deranged sponge, and once it's wet, it leaks like a runny faucet until I can find a towel and a blow dryer because air drying is not an option.

Maya notices my wet trail and jokes that I should be on one of those Sham-wow infomercials. Not as the salesperson shouting about how fabulous the water-absorbent cloth is, but as the cloth itself.

"Like I haven't heard that one before," I mutter. I have. Several hundred times. All from Maya.

Mom tells her to be nice, and I smile and stick my tongue out like a child even though I'm a grown woman now. I wonder when I'll actually feel like a woman. My body certainly hasn't gotten the message that femininity should've reached its peak within me by now. Exhibit A being my chicken legs and exhibit B being my lack of graceful...anything.

Papa tells us all to stop walking and take in salty air.

While we're both intelligent, and share the same ridiculous sense of humor, this is where we differ. Papa is sentimental in a way that's almost whimsical. He can put aside logic for feeling.

While I watch him close his eyes and take a deep breath, I realize I envy him. That he can have the best of both worlds where as I manage to live within the boundary lines of just the one.

Normally, I'd roll my eyes or just pretend to go along with it, but it's my last summer here before I head back to college and begin my new research project, and who knows, maybe my last summer here ever, and I made a promise to myself that I'm going to savor each and every minute I have left in this place. So, I do what Papa says, and stop, face the water, and close my eyes. The salt is so thick in the air that I can taste it in my mouth before I even have a chance to inhale.

I try to take a deep breath, but I can't. My lungs are already full, but not with air. I cough one of those gross wet coughs where you can feel stuff moving around in your lungs. And the air might as well be a like a salt lick because what I cough up tastes like I've been licking at one all day.

My mother comes to my side to ask if I'm okay. I nod, wipe my mouth with the back of my hand, and flash her a smile, reassuring her that I'm fine. She reminds me that I always get a cold at the end of the summer. She's right. I always do.

So much for my attempt at being a free spirit.

I smirk to myself. Mallory will be wearing her surgical mask the entire trip home so she doesn't catch my cold. She'll be giving me her usual raised-eyebrow, side-glances every time I sneeze like I've got the zombie plague. I make a mental note to throw in some additional fake sneezes and coughs for good measure.

We continue walking. My feet are aching to the point that I'm limping. I do my best to hide it so Mama won't worry. I don't want to complain either, she's heard enough of that today.

Besides, she said we're almost there, so I'll be able to rest them soon.

The white and yellow of approaching headlights spread wide in the light of dawn like portals of blurry suns. I pause and shield my eyes for a moment before we all continue on. A loud horn blasts from a passing car, making Maya jump and Mallory curse as it fades off down the road.

After a few more miles, the road becomes thin and cracked with no markings separating the lanes. There are no more lights or bars or people.

Mindy whines to Papa, and he assures her again that we are almost there, but I'm beginning to think *there* doesn't exist.

A black truck pulls up beside us and stops. It's on big, lifted tires. I crane my neck when the window rolls down. A man appears although he's so high up I can't make out his face.

"Miss, you need a ride?" he asks, sounding concerned.

I smile, and my lips crack. A trickle of blood runs down my jaw, and I wipe it away with my wet shirt. It stings from the salt but my smile doesn't falter. I'm just so happy to be with my family. To be here. I have to be happy.

I can't *not* smile.

But why am I bleeding?

All three of my sisters are begging my parents to let us get into this stranger's truck, but I know they'll never allow it. So, as much as I appreciate the offer, I politely decline.

"Thank you so much, but no thank you."

My sisters giggle, and although I can't see the man, I realize that he must be decent looking because my sisters are giggling like idiots.

I whip my head around. "Shhh, don't be rude," I say between my teeth and turn back to the stranger. "Sorry about them."

"Them," he says, as if he doesn't understand why young women would be giggling in his presence. I might be, too, but his face is even blurrier now than it was when he first pulled up. In fact, everything is blurrier now.

We need to keep going, so we can get *there*.

But where is *there*?

Where am I?

"Thanks again for the offer," I say to the man. "But, as you can see, even if we were to take you up on your kind offer, your truck doesn't have a backseat, and I don't think it can accommodate all six of us."

"All six of you," he repeats. It's not a statement or a question. I'm beginning to think he doesn't have all of the necessary brain power to compute such a simple statement.

Or count to six.

My feet ache, and I'm shifting from one to the other. I'm eager to send this stranger on his way, and I'm finding it harder and harder to remain upright. "You don't think I'd leave my family here and go with you alone, do you?" I turn back to my Papa and shoot him a shrug. He smiles proudly, no doubt at the realization that his constant stranger-danger talks have sunk in.

"Miss, where is your family?" he asks, tentatively.

I frown. I mean, my vision is blurry, but this man must be downright blind.

"Right behind me!" I wave my arms to where my family is gathered at the side of the road. They all wave back like they're a moving painting of a picture-perfect family.

He opens the driver's door and hops down onto the pavement. I register bare arms and a white shirt. Tattoos. His hair is dark blonde, reminding me of my cat, Penny. He's got a scar on his jaw and bright eyes that keep moving out of focus. No wonder my sisters giggled. He's very giggle worthy. My guess is that he's only a little older than me although his deep voice sounds much more mature.

He slams the door shut.

I don't know if it's the sudden movement or the long walk that has me swaying on my feet.

The young man glances over my shoulder into the dark, then back at me before repeating the process again. His facial features now resemble a close-up image of a fly I once studied. Large and nonsensical. Too many eyes.

He scratches his head in confusion.

I growl in frustration and spin around to point my family out to him, but the movement continues even as my body stops. Everything spins. My family. The truck. The stranger. The moon above me. Faster and faster like an out of control carnival ride.

I catch one last glimpse of my family as I fall.

The last words I hear before I hit the ground are deep and garbled.

"There ain't nobody behind you."

Pike

The night starts like almost every night: with two girls in my bed. I grow bored easily and find it hard to focus on just one at a time. My friend, Nine, calls it sexual ADD.

He isn't wrong.

Also, I'm a twenty-two-year-old man with a huge sexual appetite.

So, there's that.

After the girls leave, I quickly shower and head out to do what I do best. Sling dope. I deliver an astronomical amount of molly and blow to a bunch of rich kids throwing a rave on the boujee side of the causeway in Logan's Beach.

Once I cross back over onto my side of town I breathe a sigh of relief. The more distance I can put between me and the fucking entitled rich brats, and their determined quests for parental disappointment, the better. The twats have so few problems in life that they have to create them while the rest of the world living on this side of the causeway, the land of sand and ruin, wanders through a literal hell on earth.

Hell, or not, I fucking love this town. Saltwater and sand run through my fucking veins.

Logan's Beach is where I want to be. Right now, I live in Coral Pines with Nine but I've got my eye on a shitty little antique store on Main Street with an apartment on the second floor that I hope to make into my very own shitty little pawn shop as soon as I can scrape up enough cash.

Bass is still beating in my ears. I make myself yawn and tug on my earlobe to pop my ears. What happened to real music? Johnny Cash. Bush. Sam Hunt. The rave music they listen to is worse than most forms of fucking torture, but I'm guessing that's where the drugs come into play. You have to be high to dance to that shit. I'm the same age as most of those 'kids' but hating on their music and my lack of privilege makes me feel a lot older. Sweet relief comes in the form of Johnny Cash. I turn up the radio. "That's more fucking like it," I say to myself, tapping my fingers against the steering wheel as the first verse of *Cocaine Blues* drowns out the bass in my ears.

I pass the *Welcome to Logan's Beach* sign and spot a figure moving in the shadows. It's not unusual to see a bear, boar, deer, or gator crossing at this time of night. What is unusual is for a girl to be limping barefoot down the side of the fucking road looking like one of those girls from a horror movie, slowly trudging down the road, long wet hair hanging in her face.

Curiosity gets the best of me. I slow the truck to a stop beside her, surprised as all fuck when she approaches the truck. She spews some nonsense about people being behind her when there ain't no one there but the fucking crickets and other critters. She's younger than me by a few years. Skinny, all elbows and knees. There's a wildness in her big grey eyes, reminding me of a deranged doll. She keeps glancing behind her, clearly seeing something that I'm missing. She sways on her feet.

I jump out and catch her as she passes out.

Now, she's in my passenger seat, dripping mud and water onto the leather. "Yo...girl," I say, lightly slapping her cheeks in an attempt to bring her back into consciousness. "Hey, kid. Wake the fuck up."

Her wet, stringy hair is the color of dark whiskey, long with a crinkly wave. She has a small gap between her otherwise perfect front teeth and a mole on her left cheek above pale cracked lips. There's a cut above her eye and scrapes on her feet and hands.

She blinks a few times before finally opening her eyes, she looks around at the interior of the truck before her eyes fall on mine. "Oh, hey," she says with a rough voice, and then she smiles brightly as if she hadn't just spouted nonsense about being surrounded by people before fainting in my arms.

"Were you in a cage fight with a chicken or something? 'Cause it looks like you were. And lost."

She sits up and shakes her head. "Not that I'm aware of." She looks down at her clothes. "What happened?" She touches the cut above her eye and hisses.

"I'm not sure. Found you this way."

She thinks for a moment. "Swimming. I must have swam out too far. Mama always warns me about going past the rocks, but I never listen. I think it was raining. We were kayaking?" She presses her eyes shut, biting her bottom lip and struggling to remember. "It's all...I can't remember."

Typical tourist mistake. Countless numbers of them have drowned thinking they can swim past the rocks and the clear as fuck sign that reads DO NOT SWIM PAST THE ROCKS. I sigh. No wonder the girl thought she was with her family. She's almost drowned and probably swallowed a lot of water. "Hospital or home?" I ask. I'm a shit guy but even shit guys don't leave young innocent looking drowned rats on the side of the fucking road at night.

"Home," she answers, resting her head against the headrest.

I round the truck and get back in, throwing it in drive. I glance over to her. Her eyes are shut. The skin of her eyelids are a purple color, and I can't tell if it's a shadow, dirt, or bruising. "And where might that be, darlin'?"

She opens her eyes and sits up with a grimace. "We live in Ocala, but we summer here on the beach. One-twelve-four-four Sycamore Drive. That's the address of the timeshare."

At least, she knows her address. That's something. "You sure you don't need a hospital?"

She takes a deep breath and plasters a smile on her face. "I'm sure. I just need to get cleaned up. My parents are going to be so pissed. They're probably out looking for me."

I nod. "I can get you home quick. I know where the road is. It ain't far from where I just came from." As I drive, I feel her stare on my cheek burning a hole in my face.

Finally, she speaks, "Thank you. I mean, for the ride." Her pale sunken cheeks gain some color as she blushes. She bites her bottom lip and hisses, raising her fingers to the cut on her lip she'd forgotten about.

I haven't done a lot of things in my twenty-two years that deserve thanks, and I sure as shit haven't done anything recently to deserve it either. It feels wrong for her to be thanking me and even more wrong that I have no idea how to respond to simple gratitude.

We're silent for the rest of the drive. The only sounds are the occasional passing cars and the echo of croaking frogs from the neighboring preserves.

I turn down a broken shell driveway lined with a crooked orange stained fence and broken shell plant beds housing the kind of tall skinny palm trees that sway in a slight breeze as if they're in a hurricane. Funny enough, those fuckers are the ones who survive most hurricanes when everything around them turns to rubble because they bend like rubber bands and always snap back.

"This is it," she says on an exhale, her face brightens.

The house itself is a sunny yellow color, sitting high on pilings with two parking spaces underneath separated by an unpainted concrete block wall. Purple shutters surround the two windows. Hanging underneath each window is a large rusty metal sun with house numbers. There's a small outbuilding off to the side that matches the paint scheme of the house. It's a duplex. One of hundreds just like it lining the beachfront. Like the others, I assume the wooden stair cases on both the left and right lead up to a deck on the beachside of the house where the front door is located because that's how all of these things are laid out and there are hundreds of them lining the beach. Who knows, I could have been here before, either for business or because spring break tends to bring out wild girls with daddy issues who love nothing more than to slum it with the locals on spring break.

The kind of girls who don't mind that they won't be the only girl in my bed.

The girl opens the door and hops down, stumbling on the shell driveway.

"Shit," I swear, jumping down and racing over to hold her upright. "Maybe a hospital would have been a better idea."

"No. I'm good. I'm always good when I'm here," she says, her eyes sparkling as she looks up at the little beach house like it's a mansion covered in diamonds. Again, I'm not seeing what she sees.

"Which side?" I ask.

"The stairs on the right," she replies.

I wrap an arm around her waist and place her arm around my shoulder, guiding her over to the stairs.

"You know, I've spent every summer here since I was eight," she begins. She turns her head as she notices the empty parking bay. "The van. It's not here. Maybe they aren't back yet. Probably still out looking for me. I'm going to get an ear full from Papa for sure."

Her eyes glaze over, reverting to the look she had when I found her.

I tighten my grip around her waist when I feel her swaying. "You okay?"

"I…I don't know." Rounded wide-set eyes stare up at me with confusion. "I don't know what's happening." She stumbles back, and I pull her in close, anchoring her to my chest. "The rain. The sounds. The glass. Where did they all go?"

I've met some crazy bitches in my life, but this one might be even crazier than the girl who slashed my tires or the one who tried to set my apartment on fire. "You know," I say. "You remind me of my sixth grade English teacher." I rest my chin on her wet head as she burrows her face into my shirt, seeking comfort from a stranger. From *me* of all people. "'Cause I didn't understand a fucking thing she said either."

What the hell am I supposed to do with her? She's not the kind of crazy that leads to being naked and making questionable decisions to piss off her daddy, but the kind that ends in strait-jackets and a memoir about her life growing up in the looney-bin. I took her home; do I just leave her here? She isn't my problem. Yet, as she wraps her arms around my waist like she's holding on to a tree in a storm, I feel obligated. This need to protect her from whatever it is that's going on in her brain that has her shaking against me.

"I don't know what to do here," I tell her with a laugh. I don't know the first thing about comforting anyone.

"I don't know either," she sighs. "You're a good distraction." She pulls away just enough to crane her neck, looking up at me. "Distractions are nice."

Distraction? Now, that I can do.

I wrap my hand around her neck, lace my fingers through her hair, and press my lips to hers.

She makes a noise in my mouth, and at first, I think it's a moan, so I push further, pressing my tongue between her lips.

She pushes against my chest. Nope. It wasn't a moan.

I release her, taking a step back.

"What are you doing?" she shouts, chest heaving. Her eyes look clearer. Angry as all fuck, but clearer. "Besides ruining a moment." There's something else behind the anger and confusion. Heat. Longing.

My cock thickens in my jeans. Good. I'm glad I'm not the only one who feels it.

She sits on the bottom step. I lean against the railing, light a smoke and shrug. "I didn't know what else to do. You were going a bit off the rails. Had to pull you back in before you fucking crashed. I'm not good at comforting. Never done it before. You said you wanted a distraction."

I could distract you even more.

Obviously, the girl isn't in her right mind, and it's somehow contagious because there's no way I actually want to kiss her again. I've never wanted to kiss a girl in my entire life. Fuck? Yes. Kiss? Never. Not my style. Women aren't to be trusted or kissed. I'd take that belief all the way to the bank.

If I believed in banks.

Which I don't.

She cocks her head to the side and squints. "You didn't know what to do, so you *kissed* me?" Like she can't believe that out of all the things I could have done in the moment, that's the one I chose.

That makes two of us, kid.

"Don't go making more of it than what it is. You look like you've got enough on your plate. You're a sexy girl. I'm...well, me. I kissed you. It's not a thing," I offer, casually, taking a deep drag.

She touches her lips with her fingertips, and this time, I know it's not to test her injury, but to remember how my lips felt on hers. She is making more of it than what it is.

I revert to my usual asshole self. "You don't gotta worry. I'm not going to force myself on you. Crazy, emotional, and too skinny ain't exactly my type. I prefer crazy and willing to experiment with questionable positions and questionable men. Like myself."

Most girls would snap back with some equally offensive comment, or at least call me an asshole, but this chick just stares up at me like I'm some sort of creature she's never seen before and is trying to classify. She wraps her arms around her chest as if her scrawny arms could protect her from the likes of me. "What's your name?"

I open my mouth to answer, but my voice is drowned out by the sound of gunfire. The driveway explodes in several little bursts, shell shrapnel catches me in the face and covers the girl's hair in white dust. "Shit!" I grab her hand and tug her around the house to the beach side, pulling her behind the trunk of a thick palm tree just as another bullet pierces the trunk right above the girl's head, adding bark to the shell dust in her hair.

"What...what's going on?" she asks, sounding more than panicked, her small hand trembling in mine.

I drop her hand and reach for my gun, checking the clip. "Those are called bullets. The *who* I'm not fucking sure of." I slowly peek around the tree. There are several armed men dressed in black signaling to one another from either side of the driveway as they slowly approach. Another bullet grazes the bark. I pull back, crouching low with my back to the tree.

"Why do you have a gun?" she whispers, covering her mouth with her hands as she eyes the weapon in my hands.

"Really?" I whisper back. "Now is not the fucking time."

"We're here for the girl. Send her out, and we'll be on our way," a masculine voice shouts from nearby.

"Me?" she whispers, pointing to her chest. "What could they want with me?"

I raise an eyebrow. "You're telling me that there's a team of armed men here because of you, and you have no fucking idea why?" I hiss. She really is fucking crazy.

She shakes her head, and a tear spills down her face. Suddenly, her entire body goes stiff. Her eyes widen, and just like that, I know she's remembering something, and from the looks of it, that something isn't fucking good.

I growl and risk another glance beyond the safety of the tree. Their faces are shadowed, but I can make out their positions. By my count, there are six of them. I've got six bullets. "I've been in worse situations," I explain, watching as they gain further and further ground. I wait for the man by the stairs to step foot onto the sand. He's the one I'll take out first. "We'll get out—"

"I'm here," she announces loudly.

I spin around to find the girl with her hands raised in the air in clear view of the men. "I'll come with you! Don't shoot!"

She's surrendering?

"What the fuck are you doing?" I grate through my teeth. The girl already almost died once today. Is she so determined to follow through with actually dying? I don't even know her, but I'm pissed as hell that she's giving up so soon.

She looks at me with sad eyes and takes a step forward toward the men, putting more distance between us. "I can't let you die for me. You don't even know me."

I hear the men's boots kicking up the sand as they rush to approach. A tear runs down her cheek. "Thanks for the ride."

The men surround her, grab her by the shoulders and begin dragging her through the sand toward the driveway. She doesn't even try to fight them off. Who doesn't even try?

"This is bullshit," I mutter.

Whether I know her or not doesn't fucking matter. When someone shoots at you, you fucking fight. It might not be human nature, but it's my nature.

With my gun raised and aimed, I step out from behind the tree. I take one single step to follow the group before something hard smashes into my head from behind.

I drop under the tree like a useless fucking coconut into the sand.

CHAPTER TWO
PIKE

PRESENT DAY

TORTURE.

By definition, torture is the act of inflicting excruciating pain, as punishment or revenge, as a means of getting a confession or information, or for sheer cruelty.

My life has been nothing but torture, both giving and receiving.

Of course, I prefer to be on the giving end, but right now, I'm dealing with a new kind of torture, which involves retrieving my shipment. A shipment that is currently in the form of liquid shit. Unfortunately, liquid shit isn't code for something else.

"Why are you doing this yourself? Don't you have people for this?" Nine asks.

We're standing in front of a large septic truck parked behind my pawn shop. The street lights and the bugs are already buzzing, and the sun's only been down a few minutes. Unfortunately, the smell of grass after the afternoon rain isn't pungent enough to cancel out a truck full of human sewage.

I stub out my cigarette and shove my arms into the shit brown coveralls, zipping it up over my clothes. Nine does the same.

"Because I got a hell of a deal. It's a huge investment on my part, and I'm not about to let anyone else handle it. I need to be there." I look to my friend. "You, on the other hand, don't need to fucking be here. In fact, I told you not to fucking be here. What did you tell Poe you were doing, anyway?"

Nine has been my only close friend since meeting in juvie a decade and a half ago. He recently reconnected with his girl. Long story, but he'd been looking for her for a long fucking time, and even though I believe love is bullshit concept, Poe is a ride or die kind of girl, and the man is the happiest I've ever seen him. Actually, it's the first time I've ever seen him happy, so I don't give him shit about it. Well, not too much shit.

"The truth. That we're driving a shit truck to meet a boat, and sucking a shit ton of MDMA along with a lot of actual shit out of it to bring it back to Logan's Beach so Pike can begin his reign as white trash Pablo Escobar," he announces, with a dramatic wave of his hand and an exaggerated bow.

I tug on a fitted baseball cap with Logan's Beach Septic printed across the top onto my head. I make sure the brim is low over my eyes and my hair is tucked inside so I won't be too recognizable if caught on any traffic or security cameras. The same logo is painted on the side of the truck and embroidered on the back of our coveralls. "I'm not gonna lie," I tell him, pondering the name. "I don't fucking hate the name. White Trash Pablo Escobar." I chuckle. "I should have business cards printed."

"Dick," Nine laughs.

Thirty minutes later, we're at the dock. It's over an hour before the boat we've been waiting for slowly pulls in. "Charley's Charters," I read the name on the side of the boat quietly to Nine. "That's the one."

The fifty foot fishing boat finds its way into the empty slip we're standing in front of, and the engine is cut. The large off-shop fishing poles mounted into the holders at the back of the boat rattle and bounce with the boat's movements. A rope is thrown down over the side and then another, landing at our feet. Nine and I make quick work of rigging the vessel to the dock.

A man with a long, black beard and an actual white captain's hat climbs down from the secondary steering wheel perched several feet above the main deck. Four men wearing polo shorts and button-down Hawaiian-style shirts climb and meet him at the back of the boat where another man wearing a Charley's Charter shirt opens a small gate and lowers the steps. "Gentlemen, I hope you enjoyed your time out there today. I told you that you were all fishermen, and I think you proved me right today."

"Great time!"

"We'll do it again!"

"Great meeting you, Captain!" The three men respond as they hobble off the boat, a bit tipsy and laughing, slapping each other on the back with smiles on their sunburnt raccoon faces. They make their way up the steps toward the parking lot behind the indoor boat storage building without so much as acknowledging us as they pass.

"Boys, do what you gotta do," the captain says with none of the cheeriness he'd just shown his charter clients. His first mate is already cleaning out the coolers. "I don't know a thing."

I shrug. "So then, you won't need to get paid."

He twists his lips. His face reddens. "You know what I mean. Just get it over with."

Nine jogs over to the septic truck which is parked so the back is facing us just above the lowered dock area. He pulls off the hose and jogs it back down to the dock, plugging it into the boat's sewage disposal system. He flips the switch, and the sound of a large vacuum fills the air. The captain reaches the dock and stands beside me. He bends over to tie his shoe, and his hat falls to the wooden planks. I pick it up, and before handing it back to him, I pull the envelope of cash from my coveralls and place it inside.

The captain pretends he doesn't see it, and folds his hat in his hands, walking off into the night with a whistle on his lips.

The first mate waddles down the ramp with two buckets in his hand. He's glaring at the captain's back.

"Hey, man," I stop him. "You okay?" I need to make sure this operation is going to go smoothly, and if the first mate is about to murder the captain in the parking lot, it's attention I can't afford.

"I know what you guys are doing," he says, still staring at where the captain is now long gone.

I eye him warily and reach behind my back, feeling for my gun underneath my coveralls. "And? What exactly does that mean to you?"

He meets my gaze, realizing what he just said his face pales. The kid is no more than eighteen years old. He's scared, but he's too pissed at the captain to understand how fucked he might be depending on his next choice of words. "I made eighty fucking dollars today. The charter was over fifteen hundred, and the fat fuck didn't lift a finger. The fishing spots we went to are all ones I've found on my own, and when we docked in the Bahamas, I'm the one who loaded your shipment. Not him." He looks at the hose and lowers his voice. "All of that, and for eighty fucking dollars. He didn't even split the tip with me when it should've all been mine."

"That sucks, kid, but you didn't answer my question," I reply. I play my fingers on the metal of my gun like a piano, but music is not what this kid has in store for him if this goes wrong. "Do we have a fucking problem?"

He rolls his eyes. "No, we don't have a fucking problem. At least, not with you. My name's Joe Watershed. Logan's Beach born and bred. I know who you guys are, and I'm not going to say anything. I don't have a death wish. My issue isn't with you. It's with *him*," he grates. "You know, one day, I'm going to buy my own fishing boat, and take out my own charters, and I'm not going to treat my fucking staff the way that fat piece of useless shit does."

"Watershed? You got a brother who rides with the Lawless?" I ask, the last name sounding familiar.

"Yeah, Angel," the kid replies. A little of the anger dies away, softening his earlier murderous expression.

"Your brother would be pissed if he knew that captain was fucking you over," I say, lighting a smoke.

"He would be fucking pissed, and he'd do something about it, but I don't want him to. I can fight my own battles," he says, puffing out his concave chest. "I don't need to go crying to my brother every time someone fucks me over."

I appreciate the kid wanting to do things on his own. Reminds me of a younger more hideous looking version of myself. "How are you going to fight this battle?" I ask, genuinely curious.

Puffing out his cheeks, he blows out a breath. "Honestly, I'm not fucking sure."

I grin, leaning on one of the thick wooden pillars. "I think I can help."

"How?" he asks. I offer him a smoke and my lighter, and he takes it, fanning the smoke away from his eyes.

"We chose this captain because he's hard up for money. His boat is being repossessed. He's got to get that money I just gave him to the bank by Monday before it hits the auction block Tuesday afternoon," I tell him.

Joe's shoulders slump. "If he gets the boat taken away, then I'm out of a job. How does that help me?"

"It won't. But it will help if you drive the boat to another dock and park it there tonight. Cover it up. Then bring it back here. Park it just where it was, and go to the auction. Which is on Monday afternoon. We altered his notice."

"But I don't have…" he trails off when I whistle to Nine who cuts the hose and tosses me a thick envelope from his boot.

I shove the money into the kid's hands. "You buy it. There's two thousand more in there then I gave the captain. If he realizes it's Monday instead of Tuesday he still won't have the money to buy it." I slap him on the shoulder. "*Captain Watershed.*"

He shakes his head in disbelief, staring hard at the money in his hand before glancing back up to me. "I don't understand. How does this benefit you?"

"This was a one-time deal. The captain said so himself. He just needed enough money to pay off the bank and save his boat. However…" I let him fill in the blanks.

"If the boat is mine, then I can do this run for you again."

I knew the kid was smart. Well, smart enough. I exhale smoke through my nose. "You sure as fuck can, and you keep every fucking dime from both the charters and from this." I pat the envelope in his hands. "Except you'd make twice that every run."

The kid smiles from ear to ear. "Thank you. Thank you so much. I'm in. Whatever you need."

"Think your brother will be okay with it?" I ask, remembering that Angel is in the MC, and I ain't about to get the kid twisted in something that would piss off a member of The Lawless. Bear, the president, is a friend of Nine's and an associate of mine. Can't have my name being dragged around the fucking clubhouse.

Joe scoffs. "Are you kidding? He'll probably offer to be my first mate," he beams.

"Now, scram, kid." I point at him with my smoke and lower my voice. "And if anyone asks why we're here tonight…"

"But you weren't," he says, running back onto the boat, forgetting his buckets on the dock.

"Go to North Captiva. There's a house at the end of the

island. Three stories. Blue. It's hidden from plain sight. The dock will be empty because the owners take it back up north after season!" I call to him. "Dock it there!"

He climbs up the captain's perch and starts the engine. Nine kills the switch on the pump after he's sure the septic tank is empty and the truck is full. I release the ropes tying the boat to the dock. The kid smiles and waves as he backs out from the boat slip, disappearing across the Caloosahatchee River.

I help Nine wrap the hose back around the side of the truck.

We're on the road for a few minutes before stopping at a truck stop next to the highway. I fill the gas tank even though it's still half full while Badger, a member of the Lawless, and a trusted member of my team, jumps into the truck behind Nine. Badger's role in all of this is for protection and because he's the one who knows the manager of the septic company.

We get back on the road and head for the septic station where the manager is waiting for us to help separate the shit from the blow.

"What you got in here, besides shit?" Badger asks, sniffing the air and wrinkling his nose. "I mean, I know what, but how much?"

"More than you can imagine," I answer, not fully being able to believe the amount of MDMA currently in my possession.

Badger whistles. "Fuck, Pike, you gonna be able to move all of it?"

"I sure as shit am," I answer proudly.

"Who's the buyer?" Nine asks.

"Tino from Jacksonville," I reply. "His supply from Columbia dried up, and he reached out because he knows I have connections in Peru, and so…here we fucking are."

I put my life savings up for this deal, plus King and Preppy fronted the money to make it happen with the promise of a swift return with a shit-ton of interest. Pun intended. One point nine million dollars, and in less than twenty-four hours, I hope to turn it into two point eight million. After expenses, giving Badger and Nine their cut, and paying back King and Preppy, I'm going to be walking away with almost a half a million in my torn pocket.

After we wait for hours at the septic facility, I'm feeling even more confident as we load our shipment into an unmarked black van. I feel downright victorious as we drive off with a half a dozen barrels filled with neatly packaged slightly shit smelling MDMA ready for delivery to my buyer.

Apparently, I'm not meant for victory today. Because a tire blows, and the steering wheel spins out of my hands. I brace myself as we slam into the median and crash headfirst into a cement light post at the very top of the fucking causeway.

My head throbs. Blood trickles down my forehead into my eye. I wipe it away before it can blur my vision, smearing it around my eyebrow. "Everyone okay?" I ask.

Nine looks panicked but otherwise alive. "I just saw my life flash before my eyes," he groans. "And my life sucked."

Badger moans from the backseat. I turn around to find him laying sideways, clutching his ribs. "Yep, just banged up," he says, hissing as he pushes back to a seated position.

"Let's get the fuck out of here before the cops show up," I say. "Grab the spare." I push the door open and hop out of the van to check the tire. It's got a huge nail in it. "What the fuck?" I bend down to inspect it further. It's not a nail. It's a fucking spike. A foreboding feeling wraps around me like a black fucking halo. I jump to my feet to warn Nine and Badger, but I'm too late. Several men dressed in hoodies wearing black skeleton bandanas across the lower half of their faces surround the truck, shotguns aimed.

"Jesus fucking Christ," I mutter as I'm pushed face first against the truck.

"Don't' fucking move!" another man shouts, followed by the sound of a single shot and a wail that belongs to Badger.

"I'm going to kill each and every one of you motherfuckers," I grate, my cheek scraping against the painted over rust of the van.

My gun is removed from the waistband of my pants and tossed over the railing. "Tell King that there's a new King of The Causeway now, and this will continue to happen unless we get what we want." The man shoves me to the side and orders me to my knees while the others change the tire.

They work in unison like a fucking pit crew at the Daytona Five Hundred. Fast and efficient. Within a few minutes my shipment, my investment, and my reputation is being driven away into the fucking dark.

The three remaining men back up slowly to get back into a white van, firing a few warning shots at our feet.

"Go fuck yourselves," Badger shouts, giving them a double middle finger goodbye. His left leg is gushing blood. Another shot rings out as the van speeds off.

"Fuck me," Badger groans, jumping on one leg and pressing a hand over the blood gushing from the newest bullet hole in his thigh. He falls to his ass, lifting his knees to his chest. "Got myself a two for one, boys," he says, gritting his teeth. "And not the good kind like when beer's on sale at the Stop-N-Go."

"Why didn't they just kill us?" Nine asks, dumfounded as he stares off into the dark after the van. "Why keep us alive at all if they're going through all of that trouble? It doesn't make any fucking sense."

"I don't fucking know." I shake my head and clench my fists as rage like I've never felt before thunders through my body like a hurricane waiting to make landfall. "But what I do know is that when I catch up to them, I'm going to make them fucking wish they did kill us."

CHAPTER THREE
PIKE

THERE ARE REGULAR STORMS, AND THEN THERE ARE SHIT STORMS. Right now, Nine and I are in a tsunami of a shit storm the likes of which I've never known before.

And it's about to get a whole lot fucking worse because we're about to meet with King. There's a reason why he runs this town. He takes no bullshit.

"Are you going to tell him?" Nine asks. In addition to being bruised and banged up, his face is lined with worry. He'll never admit it, but I know he's nervous.

I shrug. "He already knows, and he's already pissed. There isn't much else to tell. You don't have to be here, brother. This is my mess. I should be the one to take the brunt of King's wrath, not you."

"You've never skipped out on me. I'm here, and if you try to kick me out, I don't give a shit. I'm staying anyway."

I appreciate Nine more than he'll ever know. He's the very definition of ride-or-die. "Thanks, man."

We're waiting for King in the unfinished framed-out addition of his house. Sawdust coats the floors and the smell of fresh cut wood drowns out the pungent scent of saltwater permeating from the bay only a stone's throw away in the backyard.

I'm mindlessly spinning my handcuff bracelets around on my wrists as King steps inside like a beast exiting his cave. His jaw is tight, and his posture is even tighter.

He looks us both over, eyeing the cut on my eye and the bruise under Nine's.

Nine is on his phone but looks up when he hears King approach and shoves it back into his pocket.

Nine turns over a construction bucket and takes a seat, ready to get down to business.

"Tell me everything," King demands. "What the fuck have you found out?" He lights a smoke, and I think it's to keep his hands busy from tearing down the fucking walls. I can't blame him. I'm not exactly the picture of calm and collected either. Owing King money makes me more determined to find those responsible for trying to make me look like a fuck up. We took every precaution, yet I still can't figure out how they knew we were coming or why they were stupid enough to hit something King was attached to. I know I'm not that fucking dumb. Whoever it was, they've got some fucking balls.

Nine sighs. He's got a busted lip and a red mark on his cheek. "We're on it, but not much luck yet."

King takes a step toward him, and I can see the vein throbbing in his forehead with each step. The cords in his neck tighten. He leans down and points his cigarette at Nine. "*Nobody* fucks with us in this town. That's rule number one, and whoever is behind this is going to learn that the very fucking hard way."

Nine doesn't shy away from King. He seems to embrace it. Gain confidence from it. As do I.

Nine's shoulders straighten, and he nods.

King turns to me with his eyebrows narrowed. "Don't fucking stop looking until you've talked to everyone in this town, until you've turned over every grain of sand on that fucking beach. Don't stop until you have a name or, better yet, a body."

Nine stands. "You got it, Boss."

"So, what *do* we know?" King asks.

I push off the wall and wring my hands. "We know that those fuckers were wearing masks. Skeleton ski masks of all fucking things. They didn't sound or look familiar. If you ask me, they're hires and not affiliated. The way they jacked us was reckless and not well planned. They shot up the truck tires from behind the guardrail, and we crashed into the median. They surrounded the truck before we could fire back and ordered us out of the truck. When Badger told them to go fuck themselves, they shot him."

"How's he holding up?" King asks, dropping the anger for a nano-second. He looks genuinely concerned.

I light a joint. "It was a through and through. We got him over at Nurse Jill's spot. He's on a half a bottle of Jack and some blues. He's been whistling Dixie for the last six hours. Literally. So, I'd guess that it's safe to say he'll be alright. Well, after the massive hangover I suspect the fucker will have."

King nods. "You said they didn't sound familiar. So, what did they say?"

I hesitate because saying words out loud that I know will only enrage King further isn't exactly on the top of the list of shit I want to be doing right now.

"Tell him," Nine prompts.

I blow out a breath. "One of them said to tell you that there's a new King of the Causeway in town, and he'll take everything from you, unless…"

"Unless what?" King asks, his biceps look as if they're about to rip free from his skin. "Out with it!"

I meet his enraged gaze. "Unless, you give him what he wants."

"And what the fuck is that?"

"I asked the same thing. He said you'll be finding out soon enough." Nine reaches up to his forehead and touches the angry red knot right below his hairline. "Then, he used the butt of his gun and knocked me the fuck out."

King thinks for a moment before spouting off our orders. "Hack into every security camera from here to fucking Miami. Find out where that fucking truck went. Pike, call up every blood-sucking connection you have from street dealers to the cartel. Get me a fucking name. And when you get one"— he takes a deep drag, blowing the smoke out slowly through his nostrils like the angry fucking dragon he is—"you call me first."

"On it," Nine replies with a curt nod.

King leaves and we both blow out a breath, although it brings no relief because we already know we're neck deep in shit. We head out of the addition and down the driveway, ready to start digging our way the fuck out.

CHAPTER FOUR
PIKE

"WHAT YOU GOT?" I ASK, STRIPPING OFF MY LEATHER JACKET AND tossing it onto the counter.

Nine stands up and moves to the side so I can take a look at his laptop. "It's a live feed from the warehouse in Coral Pines. The van is there. Now, all we have to do is wait for someone to come out, and we got 'em."

"Can that thing travel?" I ask, pointing to the computer.

Nine rolls his eyes and holds up a tablet. "My tech can go anywhere."

"Then, pack it up. We'll roll up as close as we can to the warehouse without being noticed. The second someone gets in that fucking van, we'll take 'em."

Nine nods and shuts his laptop, tucking it under his arm. He drains the last of his beer and sets it down on the bar with such force the bottom of the bottle cracks. "Let's go kill these motherfuckers."

"I'm glad you're just as eager as I am, brother," I say to Nine as we head out to my own van. I get in the driver's seat and shut the door. I start the engine and turn toward my oldest friend. "But we can't go killing them."

Nine raises his eyebrows. "That's a very out of character thing for you to say. You feeling okay?"

I'm feeling great, the best I've felt since our shit was jacked. The road to revenge has been cleared, and I'm about to head down it at full fucking speed. "I mean we can't go killing them right away. You heard King. We've got to find out who's responsible for threatening his family and jacking our shit."

"Don't I know it," Nine says, lighting a cigarette. A deep V forms in the center of his forehead as I pull out of the pawn shop parking lot.

They may call Nine the prince of Logan's Beach, but he still has a lot to prove to the men who gave him that title. King, Preppy, and Bear. The three fuck-you-up-a-teers that don't take shit from anyone. They've made this town what it is and earned the right to do it through blood, sweat and more blood. Nine's got money now and plenty of it, both through his legitimate weed growing operation with his brother Preppy and an investment deal that went really fucking south before he turned it around and was able to make things right in the end.

He even got his girl out of the situation.

That being said, money doesn't mean shit when it comes to proving yourself and earning respect.

I understand Nine's need to show them he's here to earn that same right. I'm the biggest supplier in town. King and I have an agreement, and he's allowed me to do business here. Shit, he even fronted the money for the shipment that got jacked the other night. Nine may have a lot on the line here and still have something to prove, but he's not the only one. I've got to get this shipment back or my days of doing business in Logan's Beach are fucking over.

We're parked about a half a mile away from the warehouse in the shadows beside the stop-and-go parking lot. Nine and I are glued to the unmoving black and white surveillance feed on his tablet propped up in the center console. Exactly three hours and a half a pack of smokes later, there's finally movement in the corner of the screen. Three men appear from one of the garage bays as another pulls out a truck.

Not just any truck.

"*My* fucking shit," I growl. A vein behind my eye pulses with my raging blood. I turn one of the broken handcuffs I wear on my wrists over and over, not caring that I draw blood from the skin underneath; the metal is slightly rusted and not nearly as smooth as it used to be. I don't give a fuck about my wrists though. I don't give a shit about my own blood. The only blood I care about right this fucking second is the blood of the fuckers who stole from me. I can already taste revenge on my lips. It's not sweet. It's sinful. It's decadent. It's downright fucking erotic.

"You ready?" Nine asks.

I start up the van and nod. "Let the foreplay begin."

"Wait," Nine says, as I switch the van into gear. His eyes are on the screen once more. He turns it so I can have a better view and the three men are no longer by the van or the truck. "They just went inside. Should we…" he trails off when someone else appears, but it's not the three men from before. This person is smaller and wearing a hoodie, and they look like they're in a hurry as they rush into the van and head out of the parking lot.

"They must be switching locations again," Nine says. They've done this several times over the past day in an effort to keep us from locating them.

Too fucking late.

"Our shit in there?" I ask, pointing at the van.

Nine shakes his head. "Not all of it. They must be moving it in smaller shipments."

"Doesn't matter. We need info. You see anyone else get in the van?"

Nine smiles. "Nope. Just the driver."

My adrenaline races as I slam on the gas and head toward

the direction of the warehouse. There's only one road in and out of town from the warehouse. There's no escaping us now.

We drive for less than a minute before I spy the headlights of the white van speeding toward us in the wrong lane. "What kind of fucking driver did they fucking hire?" Nine asks.

The driver spots us and swerves into the next lane in order to pass us. "Oh no you fucking don't," I grate, and just as we approach a small overpass, the one above a canal that connects the bay to the river, I yank on the wheel. We spin right in front of the van; whose driver jerks the wheel at full speed. I don't hear the sound of breaks. Nine's earlier question repeats in my head. *What kind of driver did they hire?*

We chase the van for close to an hour. It turns into a field, and we lose it in the corn stalks.

I slam my fists on the steering wheel as a realization slams into my brain. "Fuck!"

Nine glances down at his computer. "They're moving our shit. Our fucking van just pulled out."

We are way too far to catch up to them now. "It was a diversion. This entire fucking chase was a show to distract us."

Instead of digging ourselves out of the fucking shit storm, we've managed to bury ourselves in deeper.

CHAPTER FIVE
MICKEY

I NEVER THOUGHT I WOULD EVER FIND OUT WHAT MY OWN FLESH smells like as it burns, yet today is that day.

At first, it smells a lot like charcoal on a grill. Oddly enough, once the skin burns away, the sizzling of melting fat and the blistering of muscle smell a lot like the kitchen used to after my mother pan-fried ground beef.

My stomach rolls from the stench, but it's the least of my problems, and unfortunately, how it smells doesn't distract from how it feels. It's excruciating, like molten lava flowing down my back.

My teeth chatter, and my entire body convulses. I drop my chin to my chest, my head feeling too heavy for my neck. My hair falls into my face. The muscles in my back are jumping all over the place. It's as if they're unsure of how to handle the infliction of such an injury.

As the searing pain grows, so does the rolling in my stomach. It heaves and lurches. I bite down on my lip to keep the vomit at bay, drawing blood, tasting the copper that floods my mouth, coating my teeth.

I try breathing through the pain, but my body is responding

out of sheer panic. I only manage to draw in several shallow punctuated gasps.

Pinching my eyes shut, I attempt to block out the image of the smiling men surrounding me to focus on staying conscious. Unfortunately, I can't close my ears and drown out the sound of the laughter and cheers as they witness the mutilation of my body.

"It's done," announces a masculine voice I could recognize anywhere.

The scorching heat lifts away from my flesh. Steam rises from the sizzling water bucket beside me, blurring my vision. The scent of cooked meat, my flesh, is too much for my stomach. I lurch to the side, and vomit gushes from my mouth like a broken pipe. The fresh wound on my lip stings as the contents of my stomach splashes onto the grass.

The lava has turned to ash, but it's still burning. The wound is only on my back, but I can feel it radiating throughout my entire body.

Before I can feel any relief, I'm violently ripped from the chair by several sets of arms and passed around to the crowd so the men can each take turns congratulating me with a hard thump to my newly burned back. I see stars with every touch, but somehow I manage to stay upright. I still feel the searing pain. I'm not sure if it's the memory of the pain or if it's real, but I still feel it deep in my spine. My nerves are firing off in every direction, causing my entire body to contort. With each crooked step, I jerk and jolt as if possessed by the devil himself.

And maybe, I am.

Because I volunteered for this.

I *asked* for it.

The crowd parts to reveal the bald man standing in front of the towering bonfire, his dark eyes locked on mine.

I lift my chin to him in acknowledgment. His thin lips curve upward in a crooked smile, reminding me that what I'm feeling in my body is a prick on the finger compared to the pain in my heart.

It's that pain that propels me forward, staggering until I'm standing beside the bald man.

The firelight gleams off his scalp as he yanks at my wrist, causing me to see stars. He raises my arm proudly in the air. "Welcome to the family, Michaela," he announces proudly.

The crowd erupts once more.

I glance around at the blurred faces of the men and imagine what a bullet would look like between their eyes.

I manage a small smile.

"You did well, child," the bald man says, his words scratching on my nerves like a cat's claws.

He puffs up his chest in satisfaction as the imaginary bullet hole between his beady eyes takes shape before me. Suppressed rage boils up from deep within, burning hotter than the branding against my back.

"You're one of us now," he says, lacing his hand through mine and pressing a kiss to my knuckles that I thankfully can't feel over the throbbing on my back. "And I have the perfect second assignment in mind for you."

"Thank you, sir," I say on a shaky breath.

It doesn't matter that they've marked me because I'm not one of them. I'll never be one of them. As far as I'm concerned, we aren't even the same species, and the only similarity we share is that one day we'll all be dead.

They don't know it yet, but right now, they're all as good as dead.

Possessed by the devil or not, there will be hell to pay.

CHAPTER SIX
PIKE

PIKE'S PAWN WAS ORIGINALLY SUPPOSED TO BE A COVER. A business to launder money and a place to rest my head at night in the apartment on the second floor. Last, but not least, a reason to move to Logan's Beach. But in the years since it's been Pike's Pawn, I've generally come to appreciate the place outside of the benefits of concealing my more illicit endeavors.

Plus, it makes me a shit ton of money.

As it went on I found a respect for the place. A sense of pride at the business I created and the first place that I've ever truly been able to call home.

Too bad I'm going to have to sell it and everything inside of it to pay King back. Even then, I'll still owe him a shit-ton of money.

Nine glances up at me. "I know what you're thinking, and you're not going to have to sell shit. I'm fucking rolling in it. And my brother keeps giving me money or hiding it in the walls of my fucking house. I'll pay King back and clear the debt. It's the least I owe you after everything you've done for me."

I scoff. "Thank you, but also fuck you. No. King's rolling in it, too, but that's not how this shit works, and you know it. I took his money, and I'll be the one to give it back. And it's about more than money. I can't build trust or a reputation with the men who run this town if I let you pay off my debts for me. I'll pay him back."

One way or another.

"Whatevs. Have it your way." While we wait for the security footage from that night on the causeway to upload to Nine's computer, we do what any two men faced with an impossible task do.

We get fucking shit-canned.

"Hey, do you remember that punk?" Nine asks, pointing to the small TV propped on a stool in the corner.

With beer in hand, I pause my closing-up ritual at the register and glance over. Instantly, I recognize the man on the screen. I'd remember that cocky swagger anywhere. Percy Alban. He's walking out the prison gates with his hand on his crotch like he's keeping his big swinging dick from bursting through his bright orange jumpsuit. He crashes into the waiting arms of an older bald man who looks like a future version of Percy. The punk looks a lot older than I remember with a lot more tattoos, but then again, the last time I saw him, we were fifteen years old. "Yeah, I remember him. That skinhead was my cellmate for about six months in the detention center."

Nine leans back in the chair and props his feet up on the counter. "Can't believe they let him out. That fucker was born to live in prison."

"His family's got money," I say, launching my empty beer into the trash can in the corner.

"Isn't his dad like the Dumbledore of white supremacists?"

I cock my head. "Dumbledore?"

Nine waves his beer around in the air. "Yeah, you know, the head wizard guy or whatever they call the leader of their empire. Like the Hogwarts guy if Hogwarts were full of little neo Nazi's instead of wanna be wizards."

I shove Nine's feet off the counter to grab another beer. "Doesn't matter. He'll end up back in there. These days, I'm more concerned about keeping myself out of the joint than wondering why they let some fucking piece of shit white trash racist out." I remove cash from the register and shove it into the bank bag. "Besides, that motherfucker got himself locked up. He ran his mouth to everyone that would listen, and even those who didn't want to listen, about all the shit he did. Someone was bound to snitch on the stupid fucker."

"If someone ratted, then it makes sense why he was tried as an adult," Nine muses. "I wonder who they got to do it? Maybe, that skinny kid with the glasses who pissed himself every night?"

I close the register with my hip. "Wasn't that you?"

Nine frowns. "Hey, I…got contacts."

I shove his feet from the counter again so I can pass. "All I know is they sent anyone within three cells to different detention centers after he was brought up on new charges. Probably so he couldn't figure out who flipped on him."

Nine twists his lips. "So that's why you got transferred?"

I nod. Nine and I met in juvie and lost touch after they transferred me to a center in Tallahassee. He found me again when he left the system, and by then he was in rough fucking shape. The kid was about to fucking off himself. I took him under my wing, gave him a place to stay and taught him how to earn on the streets and turn nothing into something before he found his brother.

Nine has family now, but he's still the closest thing to family I've got and the only person I trust.

Well, him and Thorne.

"What are you boys up to?" Thorne asks, walking in from the back room.

"Think of the fucking devil," I sing.

She winks at me. "Good to know you boys were thinking of me."

Which earns her a roll of my eyes.

Thorne removes an elastic band from her wrist and ties up her bright orange hair into a knot at the top of her head, making her look even taller than her already tall six feet. Her black Amy Winehouse t-shirt is small and tight, revealing her pale stomach. Her jeans are baggy in the legs, covering most of her flip-flop clad feet. If you look at all of the elements of Thorne's look separately, the septum ring, the tattoos, the tight shirt with baggy jeans, the flip flops you can only see when she walks, the bright orange fucking hair, it looks like a train-wreck. But together, on Thorne, it works.

"Oh, you know, just sitting around talking about skin-heads," Nine answers dryly.

Thorne takes my beer from my hand and drains it. "Nice," she says, without prying further, because she isn't the type. I like to think it's because she knows better than to ask too many questions, but in reality it's probably because she doesn't fucking give a shit. "Pike, I did today's numbers and posted the new inventory to the online store. I found a buyer for the Rolex on pawn that wasn't picked up and Jordan left you another message. He's picking up the painting in the morning." She shrugs on her little button-covered backpack over her shoulders and heads for the door.

"See you in the morning," I call after her.

Thorne answers without looking back and with a one-fingered salute. Her version of good-night.

I move from behind the counter and lock the door behind her, flipping the sign to closed.

"So, you and Thorne...you ever..." Nine starts, but he doesn't need to finish for me to know what he's getting at.

"Fuck no," I spit. Not because Thorne isn't attractive because she is. She just isn't attractive to me. Probably because I want to keep her around, and women I fuck aren't the kind I want to stick around and have a beer with. Orgasms and endings are my thing, but never with Thorne.

"What? She's hot," Nine probes.

"Yeah, but knowing she's hot and thinking she's hot are two different fucking things."

"They are?" Nine asks, skeptically.

I sigh. "They are, brother. Besides, I trust her, and I like her, and I don't fuck women I like."

"That's right. You prefer to fuck women you hate."

"There's a large selection that way. Besides, it keeps shit simple," I reply, because it's the truth. "Besides, Thorne already has someone in her life. Her *girlfriend*."

"Ah, yeah, so there's that."

I chuckle, "Yeah, so there's that."

"So the real reason you haven't gotten with her is because she's repulsed by your penis," Nine laughs, spraying beer on my glass fucking counter.

I toss him a roll of paper towels. "Shut the fuck up. And clean that up."

Nine wipes his mouth and drains the rest of his beer. "You wanna head to the bar?" he asks, wiping the counter then reaching for another beer. "You know, for a beer?"

"Sure, why the fuck not," I reply, looking around the showroom. The walls hang with instruments barely played, the shelves are lined with lamps and trinkets either sold or forgotten, and the glass cases are filled with jewelry pawned for a quick buck that I'll resell for several quick bucks. It's a treasure trove of other people's shit, and I love every inch of it because it doesn't matter who it all belonged to before because, at least for the time being, it's all mine. "I just gotta move all the shit from the case into the safe first."

Nine flips the channel on the TV. "No rush. I ain't got shit to do."

I unlock the cases one by one and empty the contents into a bag. I'm opening the last case when the bell rings. Nine looks to me and raises his eyebrows because it's not the bells over the front door that indicate a customer, especially since I've already locked that door, but the other bell. The one hidden behind a brick at the back door used only by the people I conduct my other business with. "You expecting someone?" he asks.

"No." I toss the bag on the counter. I check the security cameras on the screen behind the register and can only make out a shadowy figure waiting by the door. A baseball cap covering his face. It's not unusual. Anyone coming to the back door of my shop isn't someone that wants to go about their business being easily recognized. "I'll be right back," I tell Nine.

"I'll be right here," Nine says, propping his feet back up on my counter.

Making my way through my office and the storage room, I reach the door and begin to unlock the intricate series of dead-bolts and chains. "Who is it?" I ask, waiting for the answer before I remove the last lock.

"Jimmy sent me."

There is no Jimmy, of course, but it's a code only reserved for my backdoor customers. It changes every week, and this week it's Jimmy. Last week, it was Jamal.

I finish with the last lock and turn the handle. The door is only open about an inch when it's kicked in, smashing me in the face. I see stars as the room fills with familiar hooded men with skeleton bandanas tied around the lower half of their faces.

Same fucking shotguns aimed and ready.

I reach for my gun when one such shotgun is shoved in my face.

"Hands up, motherfucker," a male voice warns.

I slowly raise my hands as two of the hooded figures come

back in from the showroom, but they aren't alone, they're pushing Nine in front of them with the barrel of their guns.

"Looks like we've got company," Nine says dryly. I smile because Nine and I have been through so much shit in our lives that very few things can make us feel angrier or more fearful than almost every day of our childhoods. I mean, these fuckers are going to die, but the way they're so dramatic about the entire ordeal is laughable.

Also, I may be a little drunk.

"Seems you're right, brother," I reply.

Nine looks around. "Those skeleton bandanas are tacky as fuck. Do you wash them? Or are you guys just getting high on the smell of you own funk? Because I can't imagine another reason why ya'll would be this fucking stupid."

"Shut the fuck up. Both of you. Shut the fuck up!" one of the men yells.

"Pike," Nine says with a schoolgirl giggle. "I think he wants us to shut the fuck up." He's met with the handle of a shotgun to his head. Nine drops to the ground on his ass but remains conscious, rubbing his now bleeding temple and wincing. "So fucking serious," he mutters.

"I found it," a voice says, coming from the smallest man of the group. He's holding up the painting I'm supposed to deliver to Jordan in the morning. But it's not just any painting; the lining in the back is concealing… The man who hit Nine rips the lining down, exposing rows of plastic bags containing a huge amount of blow taped to the back.

Fuck!

Now they've hit a nerve and earned themselves hours of torture. To hit me once and jack my shit makes them naive, to do it twice makes them stupid as fuck, and now, it's personal. I'm making a mental list of the tools I will use on each and every one of the motherfuckers. To make them hurt. To make them scream.

The little guy opens a drawstring backpack while another man rips the bags taped from the painting and dumps them inside. "Nice doing business with you, motherfuckers." They file out, one by one, until it's just the leader and the smaller guy left. "See you next time."

The shit-talker is halfway through the door, I seize the opportunity and kick it shut with my foot, trapping the big guy out and the smaller one inside. I use my elbow to hit the button by the floor, clicking the automatic locks in place.

With the intruder's attention on me, Nine grabs the shotgun from the intruder who spins around, grabbing for his gun. Realizing his gun is now in Nine's possession, he turns back around. I leap off the floor, grab his shoulders and rear my head back, delivering a headbutt so hard that vibrates through my skull long after his eyes fall back and he slumps to the floor.

Luckily the combination of adrenaline and alcohol dulls my own pain, but I know this fucker felt in. He's sideways, in a heap, and unconscious, but still breathing. I crouch over him. "Looks like I might have to start believing in God because my fucking prayers might have just been answered," I say.

Nine jogs over to the monitors next to Thorne's computer. "Fuckers are gone. Left one of their own like the pussies they are."

The thief's hood fell slightly off his head in the scuffle, revealing strands of shiny dark hair falling over a high cheekbone.

Wait, a high cheekbone?

"What the actual fuck?" I whisper to myself. *It can't be. He can't be.*

A prickling suspicion takes hold.

I crouch down and pull the hood off completely, exposing a long thick wavy mane.

Holy fucking shit.

My suspicion was right.

"At least, the little guy went down easy," Nine remarks. He pulls his eyes from the monitors and glances at me over his shoulder.

I lift up a fistful of hair to show him what I've found. "That's probably because he…is a *she*."

CHAPTER SEVEN
MICKEY

"Vacation is over. We have to leave and leave now," Papa says, rushing around the living room, grabbing his wallet from the table and shrugging on a shirt.

"But vacation isn't over yet!" Mallory whines. "We still have one more week."

"It's over now. Get in the van. All of you. Let's go." Papa grabs his keys and holds open the front door.

"We still have to pack," Mama argues. "What's going on?"

He answers her with a look I'll never forget. It's both a plea and an order.

One she doesn't argue with as her eyes go wide in understanding. "Girls, listen to your father. Let's go. Now." She slings her purse over her shoulder. "You don't need shoes!" she yells to Mindy who drops her shoes on the ground. She ushers my sisters through the door.

"What about Penny?" I ask, looking under the sofa for our family cat. She's always hiding somewhere.

"Michaela, now!" my father orders. "Forget the cat."

I stand up and give him my best pout. It usually works to get what I want, but not today. My father rushes toward me, lifts me off the floor and carries me over his shoulder to the van where my mother and three sisters are already piling in. He sets me inside and slams the door.

My sisters and I exchange worried looks, but none of us dare speak.

Papa gets in and starts the engine, tossing us sideways as he peels out of the shell driveway. "Seat belts!" my mother yells. We struggle to find the buckles tucked into the seats while swaying from one side to the other.

"What's going on, Papa? You're scaring us!" Mallory, my youngest sister cries. I help her with her seatbelt before finding my own, clicking it in place.

Papa doesn't speak until we are on the main road on the way out of town. "We will be fine, girls. We just had to leave. I'll explain it all later," he says. He looks at his four teenage girls in the rearview mirror and flashes us a reassuring smile, but I see through to the worry and fear lying beneath. "It'll be okay," he adds, reassuring himself as much as he's reassuring us.

Mama reaches out and grabs his hand, intertwining their fingers on the center console.

A loud sound like a car backfiring booms around us, jerking my spine to jump like it's on a string.

"What was that?" Maya shouts.

I spin around in my seat and spot the black van tailing us. Inside are two men wearing hoods with black skeleton bandanas covering the lower half of their faces. The man in the passenger seat is leaning out of the window….holding a gun.

The sound. It wasn't a car.

We're being shot at.

"Girls, get down!" Mama cries.

Disguises or not, I recognize the men. Men I've known my entire life. Men my father insisted we all interact with for the sake of his research.

Research I realize has obviously taken the turn my mama always feared it would. *These are not reasonable men. These are men with hearts full of hate, and right now, that hate is a weapon. And just like the gun, it's aimed directly at us.*

I turn back around in my seat so that my sisters don't see what's behind us. I try to hide the panic consuming both my body and my brain for their sake.

I meet my father's eyes in the rearview mirror once again, and with one glance, I know he sees what I see. I want to ask them why they're shooting at us, but I already know.

Papa's been found out.

I wrap my arm around Mallory and push on her shoulders so her head is down, mirroring the position of Maya and Mindy. "Shhhh. It will be fine. Just a little unscheduled trip," I say to try and soothe her fears, but her shoulders are shaking uncontrollably.

"Ben," my mother says, her voice cracking.

Papa slams his foot on the gas. "Get down!" he cries as the back window is blown out. Glass rains down all around us.

It all happens so fast.

The squeal of tires on the pavement.

My sisters scream.

My mother prays.

The sound of the metal guardrail as we smash through it. The impact pulling the seat belt painfully against my waist.

The feeling of falling.

Falling.

Falling.

The overwhelming realization that this will be my very last memory.

Ever.

The screams. Oh, God, the screams.

The icy cold water as it rushes into the van.

Only one scream remains.

Mine.

Followed by the most terrible sound I've ever heard, and I'll never forget.

Silence.

The nerding hours.

That's what my sisters call the couple of hours I spend each morning doing research or conducting experiments while the rest of the house is sound asleep.

It's not my fault I'm the first person awake. My bedroom window faces the sunrise. Every morning, the first rays of the sunlight flicker into my window until it forms a steady beam, heating my face and backlighting my eyelids until I'm forced to recognize the new day and finally open my eyes. I could put thicker curtains over my window, but I think I'd miss the sun's nudge back into consciousness. Besides, I get a lot done in those couple of hours when the house is silent except for me and the endless chatter of my curious thoughts.

Today, the light is waving at me from the other side of my eyelids, bouncing around as if someone is playing catch with the sun, tossing it back and forth. The warmth I'm feeling is not the usual gentle reminder of morning I'm used to, but a wild scorching heat, invading my subconscious, dragging me kicking and screaming from my sleep.

Opening my eyes is an impossible task. I blink several times against the intrusive pulsing of light, but I can't keep my eyes open. I try to shade my eyes, but I can't use my hands.

I tug at them again.

Panic seeps into my pores and rushes into my veins, infecting my senses.

I can't move my hands...because their tied together behind my back.

The mattress is so thin I can feel the hard floor beneath.

That's weird, my mattress is thick and plush.

This isn't my bed.

Where the hell...

The loudest music I've ever heard shouts angrily in my ears. The bass is a battering ram against my ribs, slamming harder and harder as if it's trying to break through to my convulsing heart. I cough, and I sputter. Then, as quick as it came, the music is gone again, and so is the light.

Ghosts of light dance in my vision. When they fade enough and my vision clears, I still can't see anything, because it's pitch black.

"Hello?" I ask into the abyss. My voice echoes several times. Both wishing someone will answer and hoping to God no one does.

A shift in the corner of my eye startles me. I gasp, searching the shadows for the cause of the movement. I manage to make out the silhouette of a large man sitting with his legs spread wide in a chair only a few feet away.

The light in the room shifts and I realize there's a window high above my head. The walls are rusty corrugated metal. This must be some sort of shed or warehouse. The new ray of moonlight exposes only his hands where he wears a single handcuff around each of his tattooed wrists. There's something gleaming in his grip. A knife. And not just any knife. One with a long menacing blade with sharp jagged teeth at the end. He toys with it, turning the sharp point against the center of his palm.

Blood rushes through my ears so loud I can hear my pulse beating inside my pounding head.

"Who the fuck are you?" he asks. His deep voice is an angry punch to my chest.

"Where...where am I?" I ask, choking on the thick swell of fear rising in my throat. "How did I get here?" I search for my last memory and, for the second time in my life, I can't find it.

He lifts a small remote from the arm of the chair, his thumb hovering over a red button. "Wrong answer." Again, I'm assaulted with the flash of lights burning my eyes and the screaming alternative music that sounds and feels more like a bomb exploding than lyrics set to a beat.

It cuts off suddenly, and my shoulders fall forward, my chin meeting my chest. It's over. I try to take a deep breath and calm myself down long enough to assess the situation, whatever it might be.

I hear Papa's voice in my head. *Think, Mickey. Use that big brain of yours. You can't get yourself out of here unless you know how you got here. An experiment can't be conducted and concluded unless you have a working hypothesis.*

"Who. Are. You?" the man asks again, cracking his knuckles.

"Please, don't hurt me," I beg, hating how weak I sound. I'm not this girl, or at least, I'm not this girl anymore. I'm someone stronger, but who? I want to scream and not because of where I am or because of the lights and music but because I can't unscramble my thoughts long enough to focus on a single on that can help me right now.

My silence is rewarded with another light and music show. It stabs into my ears as if he's using his blade. The lights are blinding through the thin skin of my closed eyelids. This time, when it's thankfully over, I feel like my skin is trying to jump free from my muscles. My bones rattle. Someone is screaming.

It's me. I'm the one screaming.

"Answer the fucking question! Who the fuck are you?" he demands. I feel the warning in his words as he launches them at me like live grenades. "I can do this all night. Answer the fucking question."

The man behind the voice steps out of the shadows, into the moon light, and into my new living nightmare. His feet are bare and so is his chest with the exception of the array of tattoos decorating his muscular chest and washboard abs. He's even larger than his shadow suggested. Well over six feet of pure intimidation. A monster lurking in a child's room. His hair is the color of wet hay, untamed, and long enough to brush over his ears. His goatee is the same color as his hair except in the center where it comes to a point it's a few shades lighter. His jeans are low and tight.

It's his hate colored eyes that have my lip trembling as he slowly approaches the bed. Dark and wild, simmering in unleashed rage.

A dagger of pure unadulterated terror stabs into my spine, tainting my blood with poisonous fear.

The villain of my story looks like an angry angel. There's no way this man was sculpted from the same clay as the rest of humanity. Perfectly lean, chorded muscle wrapped in tanned, tattooed skin. The only reminder that he's actually human are the few faded and jagged scars beneath his left eye and the slight bend in his nose.

A memory file opens in my brain, presenting me slow motion details. It's from that night. The first time my memory failed me.

It's *him.*

"I know you," I whisper, unable to believe that it's the same man. He's got the same eyes and hair although his shoulders are much broader. His jaw more defined. The biggest difference is the one that matters most in my current situation. Years ago, he had a shred of kindness in his eyes.

Now, there is none.

"You don't fucking know me," he spits. He stares at me for a few beats that stretch on in silence as if years are passing between us once again.

Maybe, it's the pounding in my head from what I now remember was a headbutt courtesy of… "Pike. Yo…your name is Pike."

"Congratulations, you know the name of your target," he says flatly. "Now, tell me who the fuck you are!"

The beach. The bullets. The… "You found me on the road," I explain, searching his eyes for recognition. He steps closer, hovering above me, forehead creased, a frown on his lips.

The moment he realizes he knows me from before this night, he shakes his head slowly from side to side and stands upright once more. A mountain of a man looking down at a sheep in his field.

His head movement stills. "I always assumed you were dead," he says it as if he wishes it were true.

That night. The van. My family.

The reasons behind my every action. I'm no longer a fractured version of myself. Logic and memory again take their rightful place on the throne in my mind, usurping fear.

Flexing my fingers within my restraints, I lean forward. "You assumed wrong."His thumb hovers over the button. "No!"

"Name," he demands, barely moving his lips. "I never did get it the first time."

"I…I'm Michaela. Mickey."

"Why the fuck did you come here?" he asks. "Who sent you?"

My head is pounding in pain, but I have my reasons to not tell him the truth. Five of them to be exact. "I don't know why I'm here," I lie.

"Bullshit!"

I'm assaulted again, screaming through the agony. This time, when it stops, there's a ringing in my ears and a vibration thrumming throughout my entire body.

"Who do you work for?" he presses, hoisting me up from the bed. I kick and scream as he forces me down onto a hard, wooden chair in the center of the room.

He hovers over me, intimidating me with his nearness, but I

won't break, not for him. Not for anyone. There's a humming in the air, a vibration amongst the animosity bouncing between our bodies.

I shake my head. "No one. I don't work for anyone. I acted alone."

He laughs, but the evil in his voice tells me he finds my answer anything but funny.

His hair falls over his face as he looks down, and I now fully understand the meaning of *if looks can kill.* He trails his fingers down my jaw, and I try to jerk away but he holds tight, pressing my cheeks together and forcing me to stare into his eyes like he needs me to see that his determination isn't a game and that he will win. "You're going to tell me who the fuck you're with, or you're going to regret it. It's going to be fun to play with this pretty skin of yours. Carve it up and make it bleed. You look different from the last time I saw you. All grown up. Curvy. Fucking beautiful." He pauses. "I doubt you'll look as good when all of your pretty parts are in pieces."

He draws a knife from his boot, the blade gleaming in the moonlight. He releases my jaw and sets the blunt end of the blade to my throat. "Who are you with?"

Who am I with? I repeat in my head and start to rattle off an answer so that he doesn't hit the switch again. He wants a truth so I give him one. "I...I have three sisters and a mom and a dad. I am with Mensa in their elite youth program. I had a scholarship to Florida Gulf Coast University and am enrolled in their science program. I give lectures and teach a few lab courses."

He takes a step back and turns his back to me, running a hand through his hair in frustration. He spins back around with his finger again looming over the button.

"No!" I scream. "I answered the question. I did," I plead. My face burns. Tears stream down my face. Not for me, but for the answers I can't give him. In frustration as much as in fear. "It's the truth. I swear."

"You know that's not what I'm looking for. But go ahead. Play your games, and see where it fucking gets you."

I meet his determination with my own, lifting my chin from my chest. Our eyes lock. "Do your worst. I'm not telling you shit."

The side of his lip turns up in a devilish smile. His voice is eerily calm. "Wrong. Fucking. Answer."

He hits the button, and this time, the music burns through my ears like a torch. The lights violently assault my senses. I pray for it to stop. I wail and scream and beg and cry and pull at my restraints, but it's no use.

"Please. No more," I whisper, as the terrible world I created spins around me.

It cuts off once again. "Last chance," he warns.

"I...I can't." It's as close to the truth as I can give him.

He descends upon me, wrapping his hand around my throat and squeezing. "That's not good enough." His eyes are bloodshot, his teeth bared like an angry animal.

I can't help but again compare the Pike of now with the Pike I met on the road that night as I begin to run out of air. Everything is fuzzy.

He releases me suddenly, with an angry growl. I fall off the chair to the floor with a painful thud. My jaw taking the brunt of it as I gasp for air.

Pike's bare feet move from one side of the room to the other as he paces the concrete floor. I know I'm going to die because I can never tell him what he needs to know.

I can't help the laughter that bubbles up from somewhere deep inside, echoing in the room as if there is one of me on every corner.

"What's so fucking funny?" Pike seethes, pointing the blade at me. He pushes me over onto my back and stands over me, a foot on each side of my elbows.

I smile up at him. "You're going to kill me." My voice is the textural equivalent of sandpaper.

"Still crazy, I see," he snaps.

I shake my head. "No, you don't get it. *You're* going to kill me." Another burst of laughter escapes me. I meet his beautiful angry eyes. "The only man who has ever kissed me."

CHAPTER EIGHT
PIKE

THE ONLY MAN WHO HAS EVER KISSED ME.

The truth is that if it weren't for those words, she would probably be dead. The second they crossed her lips, I remembered feeling a need to press my lips on hers. How vulnerable she was. How weak. I wanted to protect her that night.

Now? I have no fucking idea. All I know is that the girl I tried to save, the only girl I've ever felt compelled to kiss in my life, is now my fucking enemy, tied up in my fucking warehouse like a junkyard dog.

And she's not saying shit.

Worst of it all?

I still want to fucking kiss her.

Needless to say, day two also isn't going fucking well. Mickey's even more determined to push me off the fucking edge of whatever momentary moral dilemma I'm having. The truth is, that even if she tells me what I want to hear, the end result is the same. That's how this shit works.

I should just put a bullet in her fucking brain and get it over with. But for the first time in my life, it doesn't sit well with me. I'm not getting that blood-thirsty satisfaction from the thought of ending her life like I would after capturing an enemy. This feels more like taking a swig of the finest beer only to discover you've swallowed a wasp. It's unsettling. And if it's still alive? It also fucking stings.

Mickey. Her name is Mickey. She looks so different now, yet still the same. She's filled out. Once all elbows and knees, she's now the picture of an athlete. Strong lean muscles like that of a gymnast but with a ridiculous amount of curves. Thorne had been the one to strip her down and check her pockets for any sort of identification. I didn't see the extent of those curves, but that doesn't mean I don't think about them when she squares her shoulders in defiance and her shirt rides up high on her thighs.

Dark waves of long brown hair fall over her face. She jerks her head to the side to push the hair from her wide expressive eyes rimmed in red. Right now, those eyes are expressing a silent yet loud scream of rage and fear because her mouth is otherwise occupied.

Her lips are dark pink and her teeth are straight as she bites down around the gag. Her nose is small and straight. Besides the bruising from the headbutt and the vein popping out on her forehead, her skin is clear. Well, except for that little mark. She still has that freckle thing on the one side of her face between her nose and lips.

Of course, she does. Those things don't exactly disappear.

She's not the weak little thing she was back then.

But, she's still fucking crazy.

She's also more. So much more.

I may be feeling off about killing her, and I will have to kill her eventually, but I can't say the same about torturing her.

Torturing her is an unexpected pleasure. Watching her suffer only to steady herself and prepare for another round— it's doing something to me.

It's doing a lot more to my fucking cock.

Right now, she's pretending to be brave when she has no

reason to pretend. Most in her situation would be begging for their lives and pissing themselves right about now.

There's something intriguing about her defiance. Something…adorable. Stupid as fuck for crossing me, but still…adorable.

I trace the slender slope of her neck with my blade. Her throat is calling me to wrap my hands around it again, and I'm not sure if it's to bring pleasure or pain.

Possibly both.

It's going to be a shame to have to take her life, but this is her doing.

No second chances.

No fucking bullshit.

Another session ends with Mickey passed out from the sensory torture and me exhausted and more turned on than I have been in my entire life from one single girl.

I leave the warehouse and exhale. Dropping into a crouch, I try and catch my breath.

What the fuck is this girl doing to me?

My intentions toward her back then had been innocent. Protect her. Help her.

Now?

They're anything but innocent.

There's a lot of things I want to do with Mickey. *To* Mickey.

But now, the only person she needs protection from is me.

My inner voice laughs. It knows a part of me still feels the urge to help her. To protect the innocent kid I first met.

Maybe, she was never that innocent to begin with. There was gunfire that night. Someone knocked me over the fucking head. I always thought they were coming after her, but I see now it's more likely they were coming *for* her. To protect her. Possibly from me.

Fuck. When it comes to this girl, my instincts are at war.

One tells me to punish.

69

The other to protect.

Only one can win.

Four days and still no headway. I thought she was pretending to be brave, but if that were the case, she'd have cracked by now. She isn't pretending. She *is* fucking brave.

She still insists I have the wrong person. That she's not the one I'm looking for. That she doesn't work for anyone. That she'll never tell me shit. *Blah. Blah.* That she has a family and is on vacation. *Blah, blah, blah.* That's what she told me years ago. Was it a lie then? I know bullshit when I hear it, but there is something about her that causes a little bit of doubt to creep into my otherwise sure thoughts.

She's not the typical soldier I'm used to interrogating, and I wonder what her reasons could possibly be to get herself mixed up with whoever is hell-bent on destroying my life.

I almost admire her. The way she dares me to do my worst with those dark fucking eyes of hers makes my heart race and my cock pulse.

I get excited when I walk into the room, never knowing what ballsy thing she'll say next. Her bravery is as erotic as it is maddening.

Mickey might take a little more finessing. I'll have to find out her motivations behind her actions in order to before she'll crumble.

But she will crumble.

They all do.

CHAPTER NINE
PIKE

NINE LOOKS UP FROM HIS LAPTOP AS I ENTER MY OFFICE AFTER another disappointing yet entertaining afternoon with Mickey. He's sitting at my desk, his fingers flying across the keyboard. It comes in handy to have a hacker as a friend. "I can't believe you know that chick," he says.

"I don't know her," I argue. "I met her once and drove her home." I tug on a white tank top and sink down into the chair across from him.

"That was four years ago, you said?" He scratches his chin. "And that's all you did? You just drove her home?"

I sigh, knowing what he's getting at. "I might have kissed her."

He snaps his fingers and smirks. "I fucking knew it."

I roll my eyes and prop my feet up on my desk. "I did it to shut her up. She was rambling on some crazy nonsense, and then she looked scared and maybe like she needed a distraction, so I distracted her."

Nine goes back to his laptop. "Maybe, if you do it again, it'll get her to talk."

I've thought about that. A lot. "Shut the fuck up." I point to his laptop. "Are you going to tell me what you've found or not?"

"I just pulled some files of hers." He taps a few keys. "Here we go. Michaela Lovejoy."

"Lovejoy?" I question. "It doesn't even sound like a real name." Yet, oddly enough, it fits her.

"If you're done mocking your captive's last name…" He squints at the screen. "Holy shit. You're never going to believe this shit."

"What?" I ask, sitting upright.

Nine's eyes dart quickly from left to right as he reads. "It says here that she graduated high school at fourteen. College at seventeen with a double masters in behavioral neuroscience. She joined Mensa at age ten with a tested IQ score of one-sixty."

"Is that high?" I ask, knowing nothing about IQ scores.

"For kids, it's the most you can score." Nine rubs his hand over his open mouth, and it annoys me that he's impressed by the girl tied to my fucking bed.

He must mistake my irritation for confusion because he continues, "Think about it this way: I have a one-thirty-five which is well above average, and Albert Einstein had a one-sixty. She scored that at age ten."

"She said she's a teacher. Gives lectures or some shit," I offer.

Nine scans the screen. "Yeah. She was a professor. She's not just Michaela Lovejoy. She's Dr. Michaela Lovejoy Sc.D." He says, with his mouth agape. His looks to me. "That's a doctor of science."

"I know that," I mutter.

I did not know that.

My schooling consisted of never attending any classes, Christmas-treeing all of my tests, and finally, dropping out of high school before the end of freshman year.

I stand and round the desk, looking at the screen over Nine's shoulder at a headshot of Mickey. She's smiling and unbruised, but there's no doubt the girl in the lab coat is the same girl in my warehouse. "What do you mean *was* a professor?"

"*Was* because she dropped off the radar a few years ago. Vanished. She has no social media, no online presence. Not even so much as a parking ticket, and her driver's license expired six months ago."

"What about her family? She's always rambling on about them. Can you find out anything on 'em?"

He hits a few keys. "Her family is...fuck me." He whistles, leaning back in the chair and folding his hands behind his head.

"Her family is what?" I hate that I have to keep prompting him to tell me shit. I'd fucking read it myself if I knew it wouldn't take me an hour to read the same thing it takes him a few seconds to get through.

His eyes meet mine. "They're missing. All of them. The same time Mickey dropped out of sight, so did they. It says here—" he scrolls to an article written in the university newspaper. "—they went missing while on summer vacation here in Logan's Beach and were never found."

What the fuck? I shake my head. "That can't be right. She talks about them now, not in the past. They're alive, just like she is, and I'd bet money that she knows where they are." I pace to the door of the office and back again. "Did someone stand to benefit if they died?"

"You think they faked their own deaths?"

I shrug. "It's possible, if they were trying to collect on insurance or something."

It takes a few minutes for Nine to pull up some court records. "Not that I can see. Mickey's parents owed a lot of money to a lot of people, but they were never declared dead legally, which they would need to be for anyone to collect on anything. They owned a vacation property here in Logan's Beach, a condo, as well as their main house in Ocala. Both properties went back to the bank." Nine frowns and chews his thumbnail. "What could a girl with that kind of intelligence be doing mixed up with the kind of fuckers that have some sort of vendetta against us?"

"I have no idea," I glance through the window where my captive is currently gagged and blindfolded. "But I'm going to find the fuck out."

"More torture?" Nine asks. "Because honestly, I don't know how you can stand it yourself. That fucking music, ugh. EDM is torture enough without being at that volume. What happened to old fashioned torture, you know with knives and shit."

"Ear plugs," I reply. "That's how I put up with it. Came up with the idea after selling dope to kids at a rave. The noise cancelling feature kicks on when I hit the button."

Nine slowly claps. "I'm impressed, Pikey-boy. It's good to know you're not just a pretty face. I guess Mickey's not the only genius in da house." He crosses his feet on my desk. "So, you going with knives or no? You haven't yet answered me."

I close my eyes and imagine slicing Mickey's skin and bleeding the truth from her. My eyes snap open. I shake my head. "I can't go stripping her down for parts if I don't yet know the value of her whole."

Nine shuts his laptop and shoves it in his bag. "While I truly enjoy your comparison of torture to vehicular theft, I gotta get back to my place and handle my own problems. Let me know what you get from her. If anything."

"Poe drinking again?" I ask. Poe is Nine's girl. She's got more issues than most magazines, but somehow, even her anxiety levels Nine out.

Nine sighs. "No, it's worse. She *stopped* drinking. Don't know what to do with her when she's not cradling a bottle of vodka like a baby in her arms." Pausing on his way to the door, he reaches into his laptop case, pulling out a folded document. "I told Preppy what was going on. With the skeleton crew, the girl. All of it."

"I'm not trying to hide shit from your brother or anyone else for that matter. I want him to be informed and assumed you'd fill him in on the not so pleasant details that my fucking life has become," I reply.

He grimaces. "Yeah, that's not what I'm getting at." He hands me the document then takes a white box out of his bag and sets it on the desk. "Preppy made me promise to give this to you. Trust me. I didn't want to, but then he said something about him being my only family and making me swear on a stack of fucking pancakes that my dick would fall off if I didn't give it to you."

"Sounds serious," I laugh.

His eyes go wide. "More serious than you could ever imagine. There were cloaks and paddles and shit."

"I'm not surprised," I reply. Because I'm not. Preppy isn't just off his rocker, he's not even on the fucking porch.

Nine heads for the door. "Read it and weep. Or laugh. Or call a support hotline."

I eye the white box then unfold the papers. I have to admit the heading is catchy and so very Preppy.

A Kidnapper's Commandments: A complete guide to caring for your captive.

CHAPTER TEN
MICKEY

I'VE RETREATED INTO A DARK PLACE. ONE WHERE ONLY MY BROKEN soul and the sound of my own despair are welcome. I'm drowning, choking on my own ability to break free from the prison I've created within myself.

Save me, I say to no one because the only person who can truly save me is myself, and at this point I'm not sure that's possible.

The despair drains me like blood from my veins, taking everything I have with it, including the will to live. I feel my life force fading, and soon, I'm on the floor gasping for breath as my heart slows to a scary pace I feel struggling to beat within the pulse in my neck.

Sadness bleeds through me. Invading me like a parasite I can't shake as it seeps through my vessels.

Tell him, my sister Maya's voice whispers in my ear. *Tell him and this will all be over. He could help you.*

"I can't," I reply, tears spilling down my face. "I can't tell him. If I do, I'll lose you forever. All of you."

Despite the saying, the enemy of my enemy is not my fucking friend. I don't have any friends. All I have is logic, my memory, and a strong need to get the fuck out of here and finish what I've started.

One solution at a time. You don't do one of your experiments and throw everything out at once, right? You introduce one at a time.

"Variables," I correct her. Maya was never into science except for the time she was partnered with a cute boy as her lab partner. "They're called variables."

Whatever, you get my point. Don't try to think of how you're going to get out of here all at once like it's one problem. Ask yourself what needs to happen before you can think of escaping.

It hits me. "I need to be untied."

Start with that, sis.

I can do that. I can. If I prove that I can be of use to Pike somehow, maybe I can persuade him to untie me.

The answer comes to me the second the door slides open, blinding me with light from the outside. "I have a photographic memory," I blurt, needing to get all of my cards on the table before the torture begins and I can't think straight.

Pike slides the door shut with a bang. "Why am I supposed to care if you have a photographic memory?" he asks with an eyebrow cocked as he approaches. Today, he's not bare-chested as usual. He's wearing a white tank top with a black leather jacket and tight, low-rise jeans. His heavy boots echo against the concrete as he approaches.

"It could be helpful to you. We could trade. I could help you with something, and you could untie me," I offer. "I'm not trying to escape," I lie. "I just want to be untied. I could help you. I swear."

"I don't negotiate with terrorists," he replies.

Straightening my back, I clear my dry throat. "But terrorists can negotiate amongst themselves."

"Now, you're a terrorist?" He laughs. "At least, you admit it."

"You know what I mean."

"I do." He shakes his head, "No. That's not how this works. The trade is your life in exchange for fucking answers." He shrugs off his jacket and sets it on some sort of rusted metal tank. He crosses his arms showing off his bulging biceps. Ironically, the word *truth* is tattooed across the middle of one of them.

"I don't care about my life," I reply, feeling the weight of my words on my shoulders. "It's the least of my concerns."

"And I don't care about your memory. I don't see how it will help me considering…" he lifts his chin. "It didn't help your family."

A bolt of shock courses through me. I snap my eyes to his. "What do you know about my family?" I grate.

He shrugs and pulls up a chair in front of me, straddling it with his long legs, resting his forearms along the back. "Nothing. Just that no one has seen your Mom, Pops or even poor Mallory, Maya, or…Missy, was it?"

"Mindy," I seethe, hating their names on his lips.

He snaps his fingers. "Mindy, that was it." He shrugs although there's a knowing look in his eyes. "No one has seen them in years. Whatever happened to them, I wonder?" he muses. He points to me. "Do you know? Or maybe, you're the one who went off the rails and murdered the whole lot of them. Maybe, when I found you that night, you'd just gotten done strangling each one of them as they slept."

He's not right, but he's hitting way too close to home. My stomach turns. I close my eyes, and I'm met with the beginning of a memory I can't relive again. Not while I'm with him. He can't see me at my weakest. Not now. Not ever.

"Enough. My family is fine. They're in hiding because of me. Something I did. You'll never find them, and I won't ever tell you anything about them. That's not part of the negotiation."

He unsheathes his knife from his boot and points it at me.

"You still think this is a negotiation? That's…cute." He stands again, slowly circling me. "We'll see about that. Often, people who don't want to be found are quite surprised when I show up at their door." He's in front of me now, gazing down at me with something unreadable in his eyes. He wets his bottom lip with his tongue and rakes his gaze over my legs. "I wonder if all of your sisters share your…assets."

My blood boils. I lick my dry lips and narrow my eyes at the smug fuck. "Fuck you. Leave them out of this."

"Are you threatening me?" He crouches so we're at eye level. "You won't leave me out of this, so why should I leave them out of it?" He leans in so close I can feel his breath on my lips. "You started this game, Mic. And, unfortunately for you, this is how I fucking play."

He pushes off and grabs his jacket, starting back toward the door.

I begin to panic. He can't leave. Not yet. I have to be untied. "I can't tell you what you need to know, but I can give you anything else. Whatever you want!" I call out.

He stops and turns back around slowly. "Whatever I want?" I can hear his smile as much as I can see it. There's an implication, an innuendo in his voice that makes me shiver.

"No!" I cry, pulling at my restraints to no use. "Not that. That's not what I meant!" My wrists burn against rusted metal.

He stalks back over to me, looming over me like Zeus high on his mountain. "A tempting offer. But you look so good all tied up. Keep bloodying your wrists like that, and I might just keep you after all."

"Bloody wrists turn you on, you sick fuck?" I reach the familiar fork in the road where fear and anger meet once again. And right now, I choose to go down the path that is anger.

He smirks. "Amongst other things."

"Like what?" I spit. "Barbequing babies?"

He crouches low so we are eye level. I flinch as he swipes

his finger across the wet tear on my cheek and rubs the moisture between his thumb and index fingers. He licks at his thumb seductively, and I feel myself redden all over. "Like these."

I hold his gaze. "You get off on my tears?" I scoff. "Wow, your parents must have abandoned you at birth."

His eyes darken. He stands abruptly.

Apparently, I've hit a nerve.

"Shortly after, but it's not my past that's led to you being tied up here. It's yours. You can't blame anyone for this shit but you. Whatever I do to you is your fault and your fault alone."

I want to argue, but I can't. "You're right. It's my fault," I admit. "It's the truth. There are others to blame for my actions, but the choice, all of the choices, were mine."

"Then, why don't you tell me who those others are, and this will all be over," He offers, gently. For a nanosecond, he sounds sincere, his words holding the slightest drop of sympathy.

I feel another tear fall. "I can't. I told you. I just can't."

"Then, this is your doing." Pike takes something from his pocket and tugs it over my head. It's a blindfold. He lowers it over my eyes. It's thick, blocking out even the faintest hint of light. Yet, despite my complete lack of sight, I find myself instinctually turning my head from left to right, seeking out his hard footsteps that move in slow calculated precision from one side of the room to the other. He's pacing.

No. Not pacing.

Stalking.

"You're trembling, girl," he murmurs from somewhere in the room.

Of course, I'm trembling. I'm terrified. The sick sound of satisfaction in his voice snakes its way into my brain. His every word is a bang of a battering ram against the imaginary door I've placed between me and him until it smashes open. I wait for the overwhelming fear to cripple me, but it never comes. What I find instead of fear is something else entirely.

My balls.

"You're afraid of me," he says, sounding as if he's directly in front of me. "I can smell it. Your fear." I hear him inhale deeply.

With a renewed sense of strength, I straighten my shoulders. The restraints around my arms and wrists binding me to the bed tighten, biting into my already raw skin. I ignore the pain. "No. I'm not afraid of you."

"No? But you should be afraid." He's close now. So close I feel his cool breath against my forehead.

I tip my chin up defiantly and smile, but it's far more than just a smile.

It's a challenge.

"No," I repeat without a tremor in my voice. "It's *you* who should be afraid."

I smile in satisfaction, but my victory is short-lived.

The music blares through my skull. The blindfold is ripped from my head as the lights blind me once again.

CHAPTER ELEVEN
MICKEY

"I've made it four days," I tell Mallory. "Four entire days. I don't know what his plans are now, but he's got to know at this point I'm not going to give him shit."

She points to the door and giggles.

"Not helpful," I mutter.

The bay door slides open. Pike enters like a storm cloud on an already rainy day, here only to wreak havoc and cause chaos.

I mentally prepare myself for another round of sensory torture. I sit as straight as I can, reminding myself that I've endured so much worse and can take so much more. At this point, I'm surprised I can still hear Pike's boots on the ground.

Or anything at all for that matter.

"Hello, there, Mic," his voice is slow and smooth with a note of amusement tickling his slight southern drawl. I hate that he's taken to calling me Mic. It's what my sisters call me. He hasn't earned the right to use the nickname. He's not special like they are.

Although, he is unique.

Grungy leather jacket. Longer than fashionable blonde/brown hair. The first time I saw him years ago I remember that the color reminded me of our cat, Penny. A blend of rockstar, biker, and fallen angel…with the devil's eyes.

"Who were you talking to?" he asks, doing his usual twirling of the sharp end of a knife in the palm of his hand.

"My sister," I answer.

He looks around the room. "Funny, because I don't see anyone in here, and the only voice I heard was yours."

"Just because she isn't here doesn't mean I can't talk to her," I argue.

He whistles. "Ah, so you are still a nut job." He nods to himself. "Good to know."

I'd rather be assaulted by the music than his insults. I'd prefer physical hurt than emotional hurt. "I'm crazy?" I ask. "You're the one playing the villain in this movie. People without mental problems don't hold people captive."

"I've got my issues, but insanity isn't one of them. You're here because you stole from me, not because I'm the crazy one."

I'm so over his holier than thou act. "Don't keep playing this off like you're the innocent one in all of this. You're no victim," I yell, growing angrier and more frustrated. "You obviously don't know what it means to love so deep that you'd do anything for anyone. Anything at all to protect what that love means. You can call me crazy because I talk to my sisters, but it isn't crazy. It's love. Unyielding, irrational at times, never-ending love."

Pike looks at me for a beat or two with an unasked question in his eyes. "No. I don't know what that means. I don't fucking want to. But I do know what I'd do to punish those who cross me and fuck with my business, and I assure you it's much more than anyone would do for the lie that is love." He smiles, throwing my words back in my face. "And that's hate. Unyielding, irrational at times, never-ending hate."

I roll my eyes. "Are you going to get to the torture part of the day, or is this it?"

"Ah, the crazy girl has got jokes. I must not be doing a good job of torturing you if you're still capable of humor." His words turn dark. "I'll have to remind myself to do a better job in the future." He looks at me as if he's trying to figure me out. "But for now, we're going to switch things up a bit."

I feel the blood drain from my face as I think of all the things his words could mean.

He sees my panic and chuckles. "Don't worry. There'll be no knife-play today. In fact—" He taps the end of my nose with the blade. "—I've decided that I'm going to keep you alive." He quickly adds, "For now."

"Why?" The second the word passes my lips, I want to take it back because it sounds as if I'm questioning his choice. I press my lips together to prevent another one from jumping ship.

"Why?" he repeats. Pike crouches so we're at eye level. His eyes burning with intensity. "Because I'm going to *use* you."

My mind reels. There are a thousand different ways of how Pike could use me racing through my brain and not a single one of them are anything less than terrifying. I swallow hard. "Use me for what?" I dare to ask.

Pike smiles, but it's not a happy one. It's the evil kind with nothing but wickedness behind it. The kind that sends a thousand spiders of fear running down my spine. A smile that has been summoned straight from the depths of hell.

"Bait."

CHAPTER TWELVE
MICKEY

"Papa, I messed up," I confess, my head swimming as his image appears before me.

He smiles and points to the door.

"No, I can't leave," I reply, tugging at my restraints. "I've tried."

His eyes drop to the ropes binding my wrists and waves them off as if it doesn't make a difference that I'm tied to a chair. He points to the high window.

"Really? There's no way I can—"

He nods his head and smiles. *Yes, you can. I hear him say* although his lips don't move. *You're the smartest person I've ever known. There is nothing you can't do.*

"I can't do this. I thought I could. I thought I was strong. I wanted to be strong for you and for mom and for my sisters, but it's too much." Tears spill down my face. I've been fishing. It never ends well for the bait.

Papa crouches in front of me. *You didn't come this far to give up now, Mickey. All you have to do is think…"* He stands.

"Don't leave. Please don't go. I need you, Papa," I cry, closing my eyes. When I open them again, he's gone.

The door slides open. This time there's no blinding daylight, only dark sky.

"Uh, who the fuck are you talking to?" A young woman asks. Her hair is a bright, unnatural shade of orange. She's holding a tray of food, and underneath, a plastic shopping bag hangs from one hand.

She doesn't close the door.

Since I'm unable to do so physically, a mental wiping of my tears will have to do. I sniffle and take a deep breath. "Nobody, just rambling to myself."

She looks around the warehouse as if she expects something to appear. "You crazy or something?" She sets down the tray on the chair that Pike usually occupies during our 'sessions' and places the bag on the floor next to it.

"That's what I've been told," I reply. The smell of the food alerts my entire body to its presence. If my mouth could water, it totally would. I've only had a few sips of water here and there, and Pike's fed me pieces of a protein bar. But how long ago was that? A day? Two?

"Who are you?" I ask. Instantly, I hear the voice of my torturer. *Who are you?* I cringe at my own question.

"I'm Thorne. I work for Pike."

"Please, you have to help me," I beg.

Thorne looks me over and frowns. There's a ring connecting her nostrils in the middle like a bull. Her black tank top is short, barely covering her generous breasts while showing off a full sleeve of colorful ink running down her right arm and a belly ring with a sparkly charm that reads 666. Her eyes are heavily lined with black, and her eyes are a bright green.

"Sorry, not my department," she deadpans.

I grunt in frustration. "What's not your department? Setting someone free who's been kidnapped?"

"Well, one who is kidnapped is taken by force. You are a captive for all intents and purposes. You came here. He didn't go looking for you. Besides, my current department is food and toiletries distribution although it's often accounting, record keeping, lookout, lunch bitch, internet sales queen, etcetera, etcetera.." She waves her hand in the air.

I want to argue with her more, plead my case, but my mouth waters at the smell of whatever is in the bowl covered with a paper towel on the tray next to me. Although, it could be dog food and it wouldn't matter. My stomach growls, and I realize how hungry I am. I don't remember the last time I ate.

Despite my starvation, I give it one last try. "Please, he's going to kill me."

"Do you deserve to be killed?" she asks, tucking a paper towel into the top of my shirt.

Great, she subscribes to the same ideologies as Pike. "Does anyone's actions deserve death?"

"I take it you're not a fan of capital punishment? But think on it, because we've all done something to deserve someone's wrath at some point in our lives. I'm sure you'll come up with something that's led you to be here."

She lifts the paper towel from the bowl which I realize is a chicken soup of some sort. My stomach growls so loud even Thorne hears it, staring down at my stomach.

"You know, this would be easier if my hands weren't tied," I point out.

She sighs and drops the spoon into the ceramic bowl with a clank. She sets her free hand on her knee. "This would be easier if you weren't here. I have enough shit to do and maid to Pike's captive isn't on the fucking list. You want food or not? Because your stomach says that you do. I can hear that shit growling from my office next door. The fucking music is already bad enough."

I nod and realize my approach is all wrong. She's obviously loyal to Pike. I just need to find the right words to pierce her tattooed skin and get her to help me. Release me. She lifts the spoon to my mouth, and I hungrily swallow it down without chewing. We continue the process at a frenzied pace. Each bite that fills my stomach also feeds my brain, clearing some of the haze.

"Easy, or you'll barf it right back up," Thorne says as if she knows something about being truly hungry.

"So, you work for Pike?" I ask between bites.

"Something like that," she mutters.

"Don't you worry that this will blow back on you? That you'll go to jail for helping him?" I ask, taking another mouthful of salty broth along with a hunk of shredded chicken. "Accessory to a crime?"

"Do you worry you'll go to jail because last time I checked, breaking and entering was a felony, but you had a weapon and armed robbery comes with a price tag of some hard fucking time." She feeds me another spoonful. "I know you don't know Pike. Because if you did, then you'd know that he would take all the blame for all of this before he'd let me go down for shit he did. Plus, he wouldn't get caught in the first place. I'm just here as hero-support or villain support, however you want to look at it."

Another thought crosses my mind as she talks about Pike with affection in her voice. "So, you're his girlfriend then?"

She pauses the spoon midair and wrinkles her nose. "Oh god, fuck no."

"Then, why?" I ask, truly curious. If she wasn't romantically involved, then why help him in this?

Her words soften. "I owe him my life and more. That's all you need to know. I'm a loyal person, and Pike is *the* most loyal person I've ever met. He ain't a good man by any means, but to me, loyalty means more than love."

"Do you have family?" I ask.

"What's with all the questions?" Thorne is clearly irritated. She plunks the spoon down into the now empty bowl.

"Sorry, I just haven't gotten to talk to anyone in a while," I say without adding, *You're my first opportunity to try and escape, and I'm trying here.* "I mean, anyone *else.*"

She lifts a glass of water to my mouth, and I gulp it down in a few swallows. She dabs the water and food from the side of my lips with a napkin. She searches my eyes for something but I'm not sure for what. "Pike is as close to family as I got. I'll do anything he asks of me and shit he wouldn't ask of me. Without question. Without hesitation."

Now, this I understand. "I get it. You'd do anything for family. So would I. I have three sisters and two parents, and although they think they know what's better for me than I do, I'd do anything for them." I smile, but there's no happiness behind it. "At least, I'm *trying* to do everything for them." I sigh. "It's not really working out at the moment."

Thorne ignores the sadness in my voice. "Oh, good, so then you get it," she says, standing up and brushing off her hands on her jeans. "So you can stop asking me shit like that."

"Good point," I offer.

She unsheathes a knife from her pant leg. I cower backward, almost tipping the chair. She reaches out and catches it before it falls, setting the legs back on the ground. "Easy, killer," she says, cutting my bindings.

"You…you're letting me go?" I ask, hopefully.

"Nope. There's enough security to keep you here without all the rope burn on your wrists. Locks. Lights. Sirens. Motion detectors. Cameras everywhere and anywhere." She points to a blinking light in the upper corner of the room. "This was the boss's orders. Feed you, then untie you. I just do what I'm told. I don't ask questions."

My arms are so sore. Every bone in my body cracks and creaks as I bring them from behind my back to resting on my lap. I rub my reddened wrists. "Why didn't you untie me first?"

"Hot chicken soup to the face isn't pleasant," she remarks. "Come on. Follow me."

"Where are we going?" I ask. I stand, but my legs fall out from underneath me. I drop to my knees.

"Here," she says, wrapping one of my arms around her shoulder. "Up we go."

She grabs the plastic bag she brought in with her other hand and helps me up and out the door. The night air is thick and warm and it feels so good to be outside when I've often thought I never would be again. "Are you going to tell me where we are going?" I ask again.

"Do you want to be anywhere besides the fucking garage?" she replies.

"Touché."

We slowly make our way through the alley, passing a few stray cats who meow at us along the way. "Shoo," Thorne says, kicking out her foot to push them away, but being cats, they of course don't listen. Instead, they sit and watch us, their eyes following until we are somewhere I recognize.

The backdoor of Pike's Pawn.

Thorne presses a few buttons on the keypad next to the door, and the lock clicks open. She turns the handle and pushes it open with her foot, turning us sideways through the doorway. We move past the small office where this entire dramady took a turn for the worse, for me at least, and make our way through a storage room to the foot of a tall narrow stair case. "Up you go," she says.

I give her a *there's no way I can make it up there* look.

She rolls her eyes and removes my arm from her shoulder. "I'll stay behind you the entire way and make sure you don't fall. One step at a time as they say in NA. Come on."

I don't ask about the NA part because I'm too busy trying to lift my feet high enough to take each step when my thigh muscles are shaking with the strain. When my foot lands on a step, Thorne pushes me forward from behind. Step. Push. Step. Push. We repeat this until we reach the top of the stairs a mere ten minutes later.

Thorne helps me through a door into a dark apartment and then through another door into a small but neat bedroom.

"Is this your room?" I ask.

She closes the door and enters a code into a keypad on the wall, just like the one for the backdoor, and a lock clicks in place. "No, this is Pike's apartment." She guides me to yet another doorway. "Here, lean against this wall," she says, leaving me in yet another doorway. She turns on a light revealing that this one is to a small but clean bathroom much in need of a remodel with yellow shower tiles and a pink porcelain sink.

She sets down the plastic bag on the counter and removes a pair of black yoga pants and a light grey sweater, setting them on back of the toilet. She pulls out a bunch of toiletries. Soap. Shampoo. A toothbrush and toothpaste. She arranges them in the shower and on the counter.

She sniffs the air around me and pinches her nose. "I recommend that you do the ole scrub-a-dub and rinse at least twice. You think you can manage?"

I nod, pushing off the wall and testing my legs. They're tingling with a pins-and-needles feeling, but they're holding up. "Thank you." I stretch my arms above my head and bend my neck to both sides, cracking the stiff joints again. "I mean it. Thank you, Thorne."

Her smile is uncomfortable and tight as she leaves. She shuts the door and the lock clicks back in place.

I glance into the bathroom where Thorne set out all the things I'll need for a shower. I stifle a moan at the thought of hot water running over my sore muscles and decide that's exactly what I need to get my blood flowing before I can assess the situation further and plan my escape.

I smile to myself. Step one has been accomplished. I'm untied. Maya will be proud.

I reach into the yellow-tiled shower and turn on the spray. I strip off my t-shirt and panties, groaning at the aching in my bones. It's a slow process, but I manage it. I ball up the only items of clothing I've worn in five days and toss them on the floor next to the toilet. I'd throw them in a bio-hazard disposal receptacle if I could, they smell that bad, but unfortunately this isn't a lab, and there isn't one handy.

Leaning on the counter, I look into the mirror. My cheeks are sunken and my eyes have dark half-moon shadows underneath. The bruise on my forehead from Pike's headbutt is fading although I never got to see how bad it was to begin with. My dark hair is greasy, peppered with dirt and dust from the garage. It's all clumped together in thick sections, sticking out in all directions like a dirty Medusa.

The steam covers the mirror and distorts my disheveled image. I let go of the counter and slowly pad over to the shower, stepping into the heat. I take Thorne's advice and shampoo my hair twice, adding a third for good measure. I pile the conditioner in my hair, and I don't rinse it out until I've finished scrubbing my body raw with a washcloth and fresh bar of soap. It smells like cucumber and fruit, but any scent is better than several days unshowered and lingering in your own filth.

When I'm finished, I turn off the water and reach blindly to the counter for the towel only to have it placed in my hands. I gasp and quickly dab the water from my eyes. I look up to find Pike staring at me through the steam. "Such pretty bait you'll make," he says. His voice amplified within the small bathroom.

I quickly wrap the towel around my shoulders, careful to cover my left shoulder, although it leaves the rest of me naked from the bottom of my breasts down. I'm bare before him, open to his dark-eyed scrutiny. I've never been naked in front of a man before, never mind this kind of man. Papa has never even seen me naked, probably not even when I was a baby.

"What do you want?" I ask, pressing my back against the tile wall to put as much space between us as possible.

Pike rakes his gaze from my feet to between my legs and then to my breasts. "Afraid I'm going to kill you and that the food and shower was a last-meal clean-corpse situation?" he asks.

"I wasn't until you just mentioned it," I reply.

He chuckles. "I'm not going to kill you. Not today, anyway. I have a better use for you right now than as a sexy as fuck corpse."

Sexy as fuck? Corpse?

His words vibrate through me in a way I can't place with any feeling or emotion.

"Was that a threat or a compliment?" I ask.

He smirks, crossing his arms over his chest. "Maybe both." He cocks his head to the side and his eyes drop to my chest once again. "Maybe neither."

"And…what, exactly do you want to use me for?" I ask, bumping into the wet wall behind me.

He steps inside the shower fully clothed, but I'm already against the wall. There's nowhere to go. He cages me in, lifting my chin to meet his eyes. "Bait."

He leaves me standing in the steam, my entire body shuddering. "The door is unlocked. Get dressed and meet me in the kitchen."

"Why?" I ask, breathlessly.

He spins around and glares at me. "*Why?*"

"Why bother with any of this? I'm not going to tell you anything. If you're going to torture me some more, I still won't tell you so you might as well kill me now and get it over with," my words are brave, but inside, I'm a trembling child flinching at a raised hand.

"You misunderstand the point of torture then."

"I understand perfectly well," I say, straightening my shoulders. I bite my lip to keep it from quivering, hissing when I move the scab around my lips, and it pulls painfully on my skin.

He walks back up to me and looks me over, seeming genuinely disappointed. "Giving up so soon?"

I steel my nerves and try to pretend that his nearness doesn't send a rushing wave of fear through my entire body. "No, that's what I'm trying to tell you. I'm not giving up. I won't ever give up."

He steps back inside the shower and trails his fingertips down the side of my face. My body heats and not from the steam. I jerk away from his touch, angry at him, my reaction, and at biology itself for causing that reaction.

The look of disappointment is replaced with a new gleam in his eye. His chuckle vibrates in my chest. "Good. You seem like the kind who doesn't give up on a good fight." He leans in and brushes his lips against my neck as he speaks and the wave of fear turns into a hurricane of biology and hormones, smashing into me with a force that makes it hard to stay upright. I'm wet and it has nothing to do with my shower and everything to do with him. "And I'd be lying if I said I wasn't looking forward to it."

CHAPTER THIRTEEN
MICKEY

AFTER I FINALLY CALM MYSELF DOWN ENOUGH TO STOP SHAKING, I wrap the towel around my body tightly and brush my teeth three times before running a plastic comb through my hair. It takes a while to get the tangles out, painfully tugging at my scalp until the comb no longer catches and the knots are sufficiently smoothed out.

I put on the yoga pants and sweater shirt that Thorne had laid out for me and stifle a moan at the way the soft clean fabric brushes gently against my skin. The sweater is oversized but comfortable. The pants fit perfectly, hugging my body without being too tight. Being clean and dressed again gives me an all new resolve. The hot water from the shower has made the tingling in my arms and legs dissipate, and now, they're just sore, but it's nothing I can't manage.

By the time I walk back into the bedroom, I feel sharper and more like me than I've felt in days.

The bedroom itself is not what I expect for Pike. Although, anything besides a dungeon with fire-breathing dragons and a chain-ball collection wouldn't be what I expect for him. It's block on all sides, painted white to give the room a more open and modern feel. The bed is a simple queen with a grey duvet and two simple white pillows. One of the nightstands is nothing more than an upside-down wooden crate, housing an assortment belts and change along with an empty bottle of whiskey. The other nightstand is actually not a nightstand at all, but a safe with both digital and combination locks. The electrical switches are the kind that are connected to metal tubes housing the wiring that runs up the walls and around the ceiling.

When I'm done scanning the room, I close my eyes and take a deep breath.

Often, the picture in my mind stands out clearer than the visual I get with my eyes, and if I have any chance at escape, I need to see everything.

In my mind, I see the window and realize it's been painted shut. The walls of the room are mint green faded paint over concrete block. Several cracks run down the seams from floor to ceiling. The door is…wait. The walls. The cracks.

I open my eyes and race over to the wall where one of the blocks has cracks surrounding it on all sides. It's the only one in the room like it. I push on the block and send out a silent prayer in thanks to whatever deity made this possible when it shifts. I wiggle my fingers through the cracks and pull on the block on one side until it slides far enough where I can reach in. I pat around finding only dust until I reach a little bit further and my fingertips graze something cold and metal.

I slide it back and wrap my fingers around it, retracting my hand until it's free of the wall.

I look down and smile at the knife gleaming in my hand.

∞

Pike's kitchen is small, too small for two people to work in at the same time, but clean. The walls are white but a dim white as if the years of paint colors beneath are trying to fight their way through to be seen.

It's a galley style kitchen with a small window at the end of the narrow walk space that lets just enough light in to make out the shadows of the bars covering it on the other side. Framing the window are a pair of matching yellow, brown, and orange plaid drapes tied together with tassels faded only on the inside facing the sun, telling me the curtains are always in the same position.

On one side is a half-moon shaped table pushed against the wall, its brown paint chipped at the edges. Three backless stools with deep orange cushions faded in the middle from wear are pushed underneath. The other side of the kitchen is lined with dark, stained butcher block counters topping yellow faded mustard color cabinets housing a small refrigerator, a one basin stainless steel sink, and a black countertop microwave. Hanging above the mud colored tile backsplash is a pair of out of place white contemporary cabinets, complete with a horizontal sliding obscure glass door on one side.

The living room walls are a deep orange. Two fake potted plants sit on a round table with a broken leg beside the large window. A futon takes up the majority of the wall beside it, covered with a simple grey duvet and a painting so dark I think it's just a framed piece of black canvas.

An air conditioning unit sits inside the window, blowing around yellowed lace curtains like a dirty ghost haunting the place until someone spared it with some bleach.

The far wall is a flat screen TV, which I assume one of the fifty remotes on the coffee table are for, and a bookcase lined with hundreds of titles and two shelves of records, each covered in plastic.

"What were you expecting? A hole in the ground?" Pike asks, startling me out of my thoughts.

I whirl around to face his smirk and take a deep breath, trying not to look as rattled as I feel. "I didn't expect to be here, that's for sure." I continue on my expedition as if I don't care that I've been caught snooping or that his presence makes the hair on my arm stand on end. He had me brought up here and according to his logic about kidnappers and captives and who started what, leads me to believe that what I'm doing isn't intrusive.

"Funny, it seems like you planned to be here. Or did you and the other goons just decide you hadn't robbed me enough and it was more like a last-minute thing."

I open my mouth to reply and close it just as quickly. He's got me on that one.

I shrug, continuing to pretend to be unaffected by his presence.

"Cat got your tongue, Mic?" he asks, leaning against the counter on his elbows.

"I like cats," I reply, sounding bored. "Loyal. Self-cleaning. Affectionate. You've got a bunch of them in the alley. They look hungry. You should feed them."

"I need more than hunger as a reason to feed anyone," he replies. His lip twitches. "You like cats?" he asks as if he can't believe anyone can like cats.

"I love cats," I reply, opening and closing one of the kitchen cabinets without really looking inside.

I glance at Pike who's trying not to smile and realize what he's doing.

"What?" I ask, standing across the counter from him. "No sarcastic sexists comment about how you like pussy?"

His eyes hold mine. "Nah, too easy."

"Ah, so you like a challenge." I point out, mirroring his position with my elbows on the counter.

He grins. "Trying to figure me out, Mic?"

"Nope. I've already got you figured out." I point to the worn black leather couch in the small living room. "Single." I wave a hand at Pike himself, to his tight white tank top encasing his ab muscles like one of those vacuum packing machines from the infomercials. It's ridiculous how beautiful he is on the outside. The perfect mask to hide what he really is inside.

Pike clears his throat, smirking as he catches me staring.

I tear my gaze away, feeling the blush rise in my cheeks. "You take care of yourself. You obviously workout to look...uh, like that. You eat clean." I gesture to the unlit cigarette dangling from his lips. "But you also don't play by the rules, and you're willing to take chances, knowing full well the consequences."

Pike isn't impressed. "So, I guess they're handing out good IQ scores to anyone with eyes in their head?"

I take it as a challenge to dig deeper. He's obviously done his research on me, but the only research I have available to me when it comes to him is in this apartment.

The bookshelf in the corner is completely empty. "Intelligent and crafty, but not book smart. I'm going to say you didn't finish school, not because you weren't smart enough, because you are, but because you lacked interest." I spot a note on the counter. It's to Thorne about inventory. The lettering is barely legible. Inventory is spelled wrong, and it's written in all lowercase letters with no commas or periods. I smile confidently. "Also, in regards to school, I'm guessing the dysgraphia didn't help."

Pike cocks his head and plucks the cigarette from his lips. "The fucking what?"

I explain. "What dyslexia is to reading, dysgraphia is to writing. It's a visual impairment where the person has a hard time using capital letters or punctuation consistently. Adults who weren't diagnosed as children tend to stick to lowercase letters, plus they tend to avoid punctuation all together." I slide the note over to him.

"First off, anyone could tell me that I'm single and intelligent. That don't mean you figured me out," he points at me with the cigarette. "And I was diagnosed as dyslexic from the time I was a kid. Never heard of the other thing, but that sounds about right. That was…"

"Impressive?"

"Irritating," he counters.

A new kind of uncomfortable makes its presence known. As if the universe is fully aware that having this kind of easy back and forth banter with the man whose been torturing me goes against everything that's natural or right in the world. I make a mental note to inform the universe that I'm fully aware of this oddity and ask how to make amends.

I remember the knife tucked into the back of my pants.

As soon as I escape.

My bare feet scrape on the rough floor. I look down to see that half of the kitchen flooring has been ripped up, and there are several boxes marked TILE against the wall under the small kitchen window.

"Renovating?" I ask.

He nods. "Yeah, when I bought the building, there was a tenant in it. Had to wait until she was gone to move in and start renovating."

"How land-lordy of you. A killer, a torturer, a drug dealer, and a DIY-er. Who would have thought?" I bat my eye lashes.

"Smart ass," he grumbles. He stands straight, and for the first time, I notice something other than anger in his eyes. He looks tired. The kind of tired that wears on the soul and not just the body.

The same kind of tired I feel.

I clear my throat. "Uh, your tenant. Did she move to a better place?"

Inwardly, I grimace at the stupid and irrelevant question.

Pike runs his hand through his hair and shakes it out. "I guess you can say that if you believe in the afterlife. I don't know. You'll have to ask her son. He still comes in the shop from time to time."

I don't hear the rest because I'm cringing so hard I'm worried I'm about to implode.

He notices my discomfort and smiles, leaning on the counter once again. "Don't tell me the scientific genius is afraid of ghosts?"

Slowly, I raise my chin to see the amusement in his eyes. I huff. "Listen, I'm a logical person, and ghosts have no place in logic. I know that. My brain knows that. But knowing it's not logical doesn't prevent fear because fear itself is not rooted in logic. Therefore," I take a deep breath and shiver. "I fucking hate ghosts." I tick a list off on my fingers. "Along with scary movies. Any mention of graveyards. The afterlife. Haunted houses. And Steven King novels."

He laughs, and my entire body freezes because his laugh is deep and genuine and even though I hate to admit it, as beautiful as he is.

"You win," I say. "No more ghost talk."

"You're not even going to ask me if she died here?" Pike asks, goading me. It doesn't surprise me that he's enjoying this kind of torture as much as he enjoyed the other kinds.

I hold up my palm. "Nope, it didn't occur to me. Don't care."

"Really?" he asks, genuinely sounding confused. "That's what most people ask first when they come here."

"You mean most *girls* who come here," I correct.

He doesn't reply, and he doesn't have to. I can see him with my own eyes, and as a straight female who isn't currently dead, that's all I need to know I'm right. And because of my damn photographic memory, long after this nightmare is over, if it's ever over, I'll be able to look upon every detail of his barbaric perfection for the rest of my days and recall every second of this living hell.

"I'm not most people or most girls." My words are a reminder to myself of the teasing I was subjected to in school.

Too smart. Too nerdy. Show off. Outcast.

Suddenly feeling claustrophobic in the small kitchen, I make my way past Pike who doesn't make any effort to stand aside. As I turn to the side and shuffle past him, my breasts lightly brushing his back, I'm pretty sure he can feel the blush I'm currently feeling deep down in my fucking toes.

When I'm in the safety of the living room, I turn to find Pike staring at me as if seeing me for the first time. His eyes rake me over from my face down my body slowly, heating me and my embarrassment until he reaches my toes and makes his way back up again as if he doesn't care about being caught looking at me. As though he doesn't have a care in the world. "No, you aren't," he mutters.

"What did you say?" I ask, not sure if I heard him correctly.

Pike shrugs, "Not a damn thing. You're still hearing things, or maybe, it was your sister again." He smirks that annoying smirk that makes a dimple pop out on his right cheek. The rugged man with scars on his knuckles suddenly looks boyish, and if I didn't experience what he was capable of firsthand I might even call him sexy.

Fuck.

"Or maybe it's the ghost?" he teases, wagging his eyebrows. "Because Edna has been known to wander around here at…"

I cross my arms over my chest. "I'm not that afraid of ghosts," I reply. *I'm afraid of you.*

Pike walks over to me and places his hands on my shoulders. "I need you to do something for me." His tone isn't a demand or an order. "Close your eyes." It's a soft request.

"I don't know what kind of sick—"

"Just close your eyes. It's an experiment to see how this works."

Eager to get whatever this is over with and even more eager

to see what exactly whatever this is and get back to planning my escape, I comply and close my eyes, taking a deep breath.

What he says isn't nearly what I expect. "What does my kitchen look like?"

"What?" I ask, my eyes springing back open.

His face is serious, his lips in a straight line. "Close your eyes," he says, this time with a little more demand in his voice.

I close them again and he repeats his question. "What does my kitchen look like? In detail."

I scrunch my nose. "Ugly."

His fingers tighten on my shoulders. "Tell me how you see it right now. From your memory."

This request is an easy one for me. It always has been. Just as easy as looking at a picture in your hands and rattling off what you see. I give him every detail complete with faded tassel curtains over the small window and a description of every chip and scrape on the butcher block counter to the crooked bars over the outside of the window. "At least, they're ornate bars and have a little bit of charm. The fleur de lis design in metal of what is basically a cage over your window is a nice touch as far as decorative cages go. But do bars over windows really need to be decorative? It's kind of an oxymoron if you ask me. Like flower boxes on the top of a pile at the garbage dump."

For a few seconds, there's only silence. I open my eyes to find Pike staring at me with bewilderment in his eyes.

"Did I pass or fail?" I ask, not knowing what the hypothesis of this experiment was to begin with.

Pike's face returns to cold and emotionless. "Both."

His hands slide from my shoulders, down my arms then around my waist, pulling me tightly against his chest. He drops his hands to the tops of my thighs then higher, kneading my ass. "What are you doing?" I whisper, feeling my body burning with embarrassment and shock and fucking biology.

His lips brush my earlobe. A full body shiver rakes over my skin.

Pike takes one of his hands off my ass and runs his knuckles down the goosebumps on my forearm. The other hand moves off my ass to the small of my back, pushing up the back of my shirt. I'm as still as a statue.

"The question is, Mic, what the fuck do you think you're doing?" He drops his hand from my back and the other grabs my forearm tightly. "You won't be needing this." He shoves my arm away with look of disgust twisting his otherwise beautiful face.

He steps away, and my gaze drops to his hand.

A hand that's now holding my knife.

The fucking cameras.

A Kidnapper's Commandments

THE COMPLETE GUIDE TO CARING FOR YOUR CAPTIVE
By Samuel Motherfucking Clearwater

Have you found yourself in the position of having to torture and care for an unwilling captive? Are you planning on obtaining an unwilling captive in the near future? Or maybe, you're just daydreaming about the day when you'll have an unwilling captive of your very own.

Well then, these guidelines are for you.

Having been both an abductor and a captive, I've designed these foolproof guidelines to ensure a successful experience for the abductor (you) while keeping in mind the needs of the unfortunate fuck in your grasp.

I'm not just the president, folks. I'm also a motherfucking member.

THE GUIDELINES

Do not abandon your captive. One other person besides the abductor (you) must be aware of your captive's whereabouts at all times in the unlikely case of the abductor's untimely demise. And remember, a lonely captive is an uncooperative captive. They're already receiving your torture. Now, give them the gift of your time.

Allow your captive some freedom. How, you ask? House arrest bracelets with built-in explosives are a good way to keep your captive terrified of becoming human abstract art while allowing them a wee bit of exercise. It's good practice to get the blood flowing before you get their blood flowing. Also, the mind-fuck alone the captive will experience while questioning said restricted freedom is motherfucking priceless.

Wounds must not be allowed to fester. The attached torture starter kit contains everything you'll need to clean the puss out of all kinds of wounds, including but not limited to those inflicted by: guns, knives, icepicks, shanks, shivs, razor blades, baseball bats covered in barbed-wire, ropes, household lamps, broken Britney Spears CD's, and children's toys. I recommend that you take this time to open your kit and familiarize yourself with the contents before engaging in your next abduction. Remember kids, inflicting new wounds won't be effec-

tive if your captive is dying from sepsis. A happy abductor is a prepared abductor.

*Water must be given to the captive every twenty-four hours. Trust me, this will still suck balls for them, but it will keep your captive alive until it's time for them not to be.

*After four days, food must be offered to your captive. Think healthy and nutritious. Attached, you'll find the FDA guidelines and regulations for a healthy diet. If you're reading this in email format, I've included links to some of my favorite thirty minutes or less recipes sure to please in any imprisoned-against-their-will situation. Try the pancakes. Yum!

*Any captive held longer than a period of one week must be either killed when the clock strikes midnight on the 5th day or welcomed into the family with open arms. All information about wedding dates and times can be posted on my shared KNOT.COM website. You'll also find that I made pre-filled wedding registry templates available to you from Amazon, Home Depot, Kinkyshit-R-Us and Weapons Depot, just to get you started.

*Don't forget the most important rule of all. Have fun! Make this kidnapping a pleasant experience, one you'll want to remember for years to come. So, get creative! Express yourself while expelling your inner demons at the expense of your captive. Remember, just because your captive isn't enjoying himself/herself, doesn't mean that you can't. They're fucked, but you won't be if you follow the aforementioned guidelines.

That's all, folks.

Remember to help control the pet population, and have your pets spayed or neutered.

Word to your mother,
Samuel Motherfucking Clearwater a.k.a. "Preppy"

CHAPTER FOURTEEN
MICKEY

"Who wrote this?" I ask, staring down at the words I can't believe actually exist or that they were just sitting on the passenger seat of Pike's truck. "A Kidnapper's Commandments?"

Pike sighs and turns the wheel. We hit a pothole, and I crush the pages in my hand. "A friend of mine wrote it. He's…been through some shit."

"Clearly," I reply, shaking the crinkled pages at him. So, his friends are just like him. Apparently, kidnapping is such a regular thing with them that he found the need to write out guidelines.

"You think that's bad, you should see the fucking kit," Pike remarks, rolling down his window and lighting a cigarette.

Realizing I have no idea where we're going, I grow nervous. "Is this when you start using me as bait?"

"No, that will start back at the pawn shop. I'll have you sit in the storefront with Thorne. People talk in this town, and if I'm right, then they'll talk about you. The more people talk, the more word gets around, the more likely your people will know you're alive and be coming for you." He looks over at me. "And I'll be ready."

"They're not my people," I mutter.

"What was that?" he asks.

"Absolutely nothing," I grumble, staring out the window as the road we're on grows narrower and the buildings fewer and farther between as we drive further away from Logan's Beach. Soon, I'm feeling claustrophobic as overgrown brush reaches out from both sides, as if frozen in the middle of trying to swallow us whole.

One of the truck tires dips into a large pothole. I grab hold onto the 'oh shit' handle above me to protect my head from colliding with the headliner. "Where are you taking me?" I ask, feeling more and more unease. We've long passed civilization and are entering what looks like banjo country.

Pike turns off the sparsely paved road onto a dirt one that's even bumpier. My butt lifts off then slams back down on the seat several times. We pass under a canopy of trees arching across the road above our heads. Through the leaves, the setting sun twinkles like a thousand pink and orange stars, shedding beauty on an otherwise ominous moment.

"Gotta meet someone," Pike replies, looking out the windshield appearing lost in thought.

"Why are you taking me with you?"

"What's with all of the fucking questions?" he asks.

"Maybe, you're not the only one who likes to torture people?" I say sarcastically.

That earns me an eyeroll and a twitch of his lips which I'm learning he does when he's trying not to smile. "Because after the knife bullshit, I don't trust you not to try shit, and I can't have you trying to stab the help during business hours."

I shrug. His reasonings aren't off the mark. I would do the same if I were him. Although, he doesn't have to know that I wouldn't stab Thorne. Unless, of course, she tried to stab me first. In which case, game on.

Pike parks the truck in the middle of the road and gets out.

"What if someone wants to pass us?" I call after him.

He doesn't turn around. "Nobody comes out here," he replies.

Nobody comes out here.

Pike turns around and sees I'm not following. "You coming, or you gonna stay here and get eaten by the critters?"

I cross my arms over my chest. "It's better than going with you and getting fed to the critters," I argue.

Pike strides over to me and lifts my chin with his fingers. I jerk it away. "If I wanted to kill you…"

I raise my eyebrows.

"If I wanted to kill you *today*, I have a thousand spots better than this to dump your little body, and besides, you'd already be dead before I dragged you all the way out here."

If his words are meant to comfort me, they fail. "Why would I already be dead?" I ask, seeking a logical answer to his absurd statement.

Pike answers as if it's obvious and he can't believe he has to explain this to me. "No one wants to drive all the way out here to a place like this with a screamer in the trunk." He turns and walks down a narrow path

I hesitate, looking around. The sun is almost set, and the bugs are chirping and buzzing all around me. A toad croaks. An owl hoots. A coyote…*shit.*

I jog to catch up to Pike who chuckles under his breath. I don't want to admit it, but the situation is funny, if only because it's also ridiculous. I'm voluntarily seeking safety from the critters and creatures with Pike, of all people, when running into a field of coyotes would probably be the safer choice. But even logical people have illogical moments, and obviously this is one of mine, and one of many when it comes to Pike.

"Who, exactly, are you meeting out in the middle of

nowhere?" I ask, wondering what type of person would come out here of their own free will.

Well, besides Pike.

Pike pauses as we come to a small clearing with a shallow swamp-like pond in the middle surrounded by tall grass. "That's who." He points to a man standing on an airboat about twenty feet away.

Dirt covers the man's sunken cheeks along with his overalls and what I assume used to be a white tank top underneath. He spots us and smiles, accentuating the wrinkles around his tanned and leathery lips and eyes. A smattering of long white whiskers hangs from a pointed chin. He covers his lips with his index finger indicating that we should be quiet then looks down with determination to something at the bow of the boat. He doesn't look like a person in the middle of the swamp, but more like a part of it. Like a frog or tree. He's just supposed to be here.

I strain my neck to see what it is that has the man so fixated, but I can't see anything in front of the boat. "What's he doing?"

"Just watch," Pike whispers.

The man grabs what looks like a paint roller stick but without the roller part on the metal hook. After a few motionless minutes, he suddenly stabs it into a patch of tall grass. I startle at the sudden movement. He kneels and grabs something with his hand, his muscles tight with the exertion it takes to do whatever it is he's doing. Dropping the paint stick, he reaches his now free hand to grab a burlap sack.

He rises up and begins to feed something into the bag. A very big and long slithering something.

"Is that a...snake?" I ask, noticing the shiny beige, brown, and yellow pattern on its skin.

"Python!" the man announces triumphantly. I guess we don't have to be quiet anymore. His smile reveals a missing front tooth.

A python? I search my brain for any files on pythons, and the only bit of information I come up with is that they aren't native to this area.

"That's Gutter," Pike explains.

He continues to feed the snake's body into the bag for what seems like an eternity. It has to be at least twelve feet long. It's thick, too. My hands wouldn't even touch if I grabbed it. I shudder at the thought of actually laying my hands on it, and I'm relieved when the snake is fully in the bag. He ties it up and places the bag inside yet another bag, tying it shut at the top, but he's not done yet. He grabs a back roll of electrical tape, wrapping it around the bag several times before cutting it with his teeth and setting the snake inside a square containment area at the front of the boat. Gutter then turns a handle on the trolling motor of the boat and makes his way toward us, beaching the boat on the mud only a foot or two away.

Gutter plops down at the edge of the boat and greets us with a slight tip of the brim of his ball cap. Now that he's closer, I can read what it says, *Willie Nelson 2020.*

I lean over the edge of the boat and glance at the bag containing the snake, fascinated with why it's there and the expertise in which Gutter had caught him. I have a million questions filling my mind, yet I'm not sure which to start with. All I know is that I need information more than I need to breathe.

Gutter snaps his fingers. "Oh, I almost forgot something." He takes a sheet of paper out of the front pocket of his overalls and peels something from it, slapping it over the tape on the bag. It's a sticker with his picture on it. He's smiling and doing a double thumbs up. The caption below reads BAGGED AND TAGGED BY GUTTER. DANGEROUS REPTILE INSIDE. "That's my third one today, and it's a whopper, too."

"Three of them?" I gasp then look around my feet. "How many are out here?"

The man shrugs. "Here in the Everglades?" He scratches the long wiry whiskers on his chin. "Hundreds of thousands, I reckon."

"But pythons aren't native to Southwest Florida…" I muse.

Gutter smiles, and gives Pike a look that says he's impressed. "You're right. They ain't native, and they've got no real predators to thin them out. People just started dumping them out here when they got too big to keep as pets. I even saw one trying to swallow a decent-sized gator a while back. Anyway, Uncle Sam pays a pretty penny for each one I bring in."

That's nice and all, but my thoughts are still stuck on *Hundreds of thousands.*

Pike lights a cigarette. "Selling out with a government job after all, huh, Gutter?" .

Gutter rolls his eyes. "Fuck you, Pike. Everyone around these parts knows I ain't no government employee and won't ever be." He spits on the ground next to his feet to punctuate his point. "Just benefiting off the fuckers for shit I'd do even if they wasn't paying me to do it."

"Whatever lets you sleep at night, buddy." Pike pats him on the shoulder, and Gutter slaps his hand away. Whatever the relationship is between the men, it's a comfortable one. I don't imagine Pike wouldn't retaliate a slap from someone he wasn't comfortable with, no matter how playful it was indended.

Gutter looks at me, crosses his arm over his chest, and then dips into a dramatic bow. "And who might this beautiful young lady be?" he asks, standing straight he throws me a wink.

"Mickey, this is Gutter. Gutter, this is Mickey."

"Mickey, like the mouse?" he teases.

I smile, but I can't help it. Gutter's personality is either infectious, or I'm in dire need of human contact that isn't tied in a knot of threats. "Mickey like Michaela, but yeah, also like the mouse."

Gutter scratches his chin. "Michaela works better for me. Never did care for that mouse being as that Disney feller was a fuckin' Nazi," he says, like it's common knowledge.

"Really?" Pike scoffs. "You gotta drag Walt Disney's name into the mud?"

"It's true," I say in Gutter's defense.

Pike raises his eyebrows.

I explain. "It's a known fact that Disney attended meetings of a pro-Nazi organization in the 1930's, and it's rumored that he and entertained Himmler, Hitler's second in command, at Disney World when it first opened, although that's never been proven. So, Gutter's not entirely wrong although." I look to Gutter. "No offense, not entirely right either."

"None taken!" he says cheerily. "I like this girl, Pike. Feel free to bring her out here more often. Now, tell me your thoughts on that feller in Hollywood that I know is a secret Russian spy."

"Who?" I ask, not knowing who he could be talking about.

Gutter purses his lips. "That no good John Stamos, that's who."

I laugh and look over Gutter's shoulder to Pike whose lip is doing the twitchy thing again. "I haven't heard anything about him, but I'll let you know if I do."

"You do that, kid." He slaps Pike on the shoulder. "Now, what brings the likes of you all the fuckin' way out here to see an old feller like me?"

Pike lights another cigarette and hands one to Gutter who takes it with a thankful nod. "Much obliged, young man."

Gutter looks from Pike to me, then back to Pike again. "You out here to dump a body?" He points at me with his cigarette. "'Cause she still looks a bit alive, so I think yer fuckin' this one up, kid. And she's too pretty to feed to the gators." He flashes me a wink.

Pike rolls his eyes. "I'm here to bring you this." He passes an envelope to Gutter who then tucks it into his pocket. "You ain't need to be doin' this all the time, kid. We've been over this."

Pike scoffs. "I don't need to do any of the shit I do. It don't stop me from doing it."

Gutter chuckles. "The fucking apocalypse couldn't stop you when you set your mind to something, kid. I should know better by now."

Gutter hands me a beer. I sit on the edge of the boat as Pike and Gutter tinker with his motor. "Don't let yer limbs dangle," Gutter says, coming to sit beside me. "Unless you got boots on like these," he taps the scuffed white plastic boots that cover the legs of his overalls all the way to his knees. "That's how we catch gators, by hanging the bait over the water."

Pike flashes me an amused look.

"Good to know," I mutter, lifting my feet onto the boat. I cross my legs underneath me, tucking them in tight.

Pike is still tinkering with the motor, occasionally swearing under his breath when Gutter takes a seat beside me.

"Have you known Pike long?" I ask, taking a swig of my cold beer. The bubbles tickle my throat on the way down.

Gutter nods. "Yep. Since before he sprouted hair on his balls. Found his little skinny ass shivering in the reeds one night, and although I kept telling the runt not to come back—" he points behind his shoulder with his beer bottle. "—obviously the kid don't listen for shit."

No, he doesn't. I look at Pike who has removed his shirt. His muscles strain and flex as he works on the motor, his skin gleaming with sweat, making his tattoos look animated under the light of the moon. I shiver, and it's probably the drip from the condensation on the bottle falling onto my leg because that's the only thing it could be.

Gutter nudges my shoulder, bringing me back from my

thoughts. "Sorry, I'm just trying to picture Pike ever being little, skinny, or a runt."

He chuckles. "Sure, that's what you were doing."

I take another sip of my beer, trying to cover my blush with the bottle.

"Pike's a good kid. He can be a terrible human being but a good fuckin kid." Gutter says although I'm not sure what distinguishes the two. "The two aren't separate."

"I haven't seen a lot of the good side," I admit.

"You're alive, ain't ya?" Gutter asks. "You're on it if you ask me."

"Only because I'm a part of his dastardlier plans," I argue.

"Yeah, you keep telling yourself that." Gutter takes the envelope that Pike had given him out of his pocket and hands it to me.

I turn it over in my hands. "What is this?"

Gutter points with his eyes to the envelope. "That's the thing about envelopes. You have to open them to find out."

It isn't sealed, the flap just folded inside. I tug it free. I'm not sure what I expect to find, but when I pull out the contents. It's money, and not just a little. There has to be at least a few thousand dollars' worth of hundreds inside. I tuck the flap back in and hand it to Gutter. He opens it again, removing something from behind the bills before again tucking it safely into the pocket of his overalls.

"So, he gives you money?" I ask, stating the obvious and not asking the more important question of why.

Gutter takes a swig of his beer, then tosses it back into the boat behind him. He reaches for two more from the cooler and pops the tops of both, pushing one into my hand. "Pike's been giving me money for years. He says it's a debt he's paying on account of me saving his life or some shit, but I can't get him to stop. Even threatened to burn it once, and he threatened to buy me a damned house if I didn't keep it." He sighs and looks to his hands where he's holding what I can see now is a picture. "But this here isn't about a debt." He hands me the picture. It's of a woman and a man holding a baby in their arms. "It's about kindness, even though the lord knows I don't deserve it."

The couple looks to be in their late twenties. They're smiling down at the baby between them with love shining in their eyes. "Who are they?"

He points to the picture. "That, there, is my daughter, Edie and her husband, Glen. That's my granddaughter, Julia." He rubs a dirt caked finger over her little chubby face. "I did a lot of bad shit in my life. Not to them specifically, but it affected them for sure." Gutter sighs, his voice laced in regret. "Dumb shit that cost me my little girl." He waves his hand dismissing his emotions, explaining with a simple, "There was no contact order and such in place back then. Haven't spoken a word to her since she was eight years old."

My logic requires me to ask the obvious question. "Why don't you try and make contact?"

Gutter shakes his head. "That boat sunk a long time ago, and it takes a man to know when the people he loves are truly better without him. But these pictures…" He smiles down at it once more. "They make an old man happy to know that they're okay. That they're happy. Even if I had nothing to do with that happiness."

I open my mouth to argue, feeling the need to tell him something that would make him feel better, but Gutter holds up his hands, cutting me off before I can get a word out. "I'm not saying that for a rebuttal or for flattery, kiddo. I'm not a goddamned democrat. I'm saying it because it's true."

"So, Pike brings you pictures of your family…?" It's not quite a question.

Gutter looks back at Pike who wipes the sweat from his

brow with his forearm. He casts a quick glance our way before kneeling back over the motor.

"One day, I told him I'd like to see them again, not in person because it's best not to drag the past out of the swamp out of season, but maybe in a picture. I don't have the internets out here, and I'm not about to go somewhere and sign up for the social medias and have the fucking Russians monitor my every fucking move." He gives a middle finger to the sky.

I raise an eyebrow.

"Russian satellites," he explains.

"So, he prints pictures out from social media and brings them to you?"

Gutter chuckles, "Something like that." He tucks the picture back in his pocket and pats the fabric. "He don't need to bring me no goddamned money, but this...this is like bringing an old man back a little piece of his broken heart."

My heart squeezes for Gutter as his eyes glass over with unshed tears. He takes another swig of his beer and shakes his head as if to shake off a lifetime of regret. "Now," he says, slapping his thigh with his hand. "Let's talk about you. Tell me everything."

I pause with my beer halfway to my lips. "Everything?"

He nudges my shoulder with his. "Yep, everything that's happened to bring you to Pike and to be sitting your pretty ass on my snake boat in the middle of the goddamned swamp."

At first, I think he's joking, but there's no laughter on his face as he stares at me with a serious kind of intensity. "Go on, girl. I ain't done nothing good enough in my life to be worth the honor of judging anyone else, so don't you be worried about that." He looks back over his shoulder at Pike. "Besides, the rate that boy's fucking up my motor, we might be here all night."

With nothing but time on our hands and the call of the frogs and crickets surrounding us, I tell him everything.

Well, *almost* everything.

I leave out the information Pike so desperately wants, amongst other things that could hinder my plans.

After all, I have an IQ of one sixty.

I'm not fucking stupid.

CHAPTER FIFTEEN
PIKE

A<small>FTER</small> I <small>FIX</small> G<small>UTTER'S</small> <small>MOTOR, WE TAKE THE BOAT A FEW MINUTES</small> deeper into the Everglades to where Gutter's houseboat is anchored. It's a tiny one-room shack on a raft with tin sides and a thrown away set of closet doors that lead inside. Two bundles of thick sticks are tied to each side of the entry forming a redneck archway. Above the porch hangs the skull of a gator with the skeleton of a large bird in its mouth.

"It ain't much, kid, but it's home," Gutter says, extending his hand to Mickey.

She looks over the small shack and smiles. "It's very…you."

He tips his hat to her. "Imma take that as a compliment."

"It was meant as one," she responds.

Gutter smiles his missing tooth smile. "Why don't you go inside. There's running water and more beers in the cooler by the table. Imma have me a little chit chat out here with your man."

We exchange looks, but neither of us correct him. I jerk my chin to her, and she disappears inside.

Gutter wastes no time, turning to me with his thumbs under the suspenders of his overalls. He rocks on his heels. "What in the name of Merle Haggard have you gotten yourself into with this girl?"

I sigh, straddling a broken chair on the deck.

Gutter pulls up a folding chair with a large tear on the back and takes a seat next to me. For a moment, we both stare over the black water. The glowing greenish yellow eyes of a gator appear a few feet away before it disappears into the reeds. An animal turned supper for another animal higher up the food chain echoing over the long grass.

"She tell you everything?" I ask.

Gutter nods. "She told me some things but can't be sure it's everything because I ain't her." He takes a swig of his beer. "I'm assuming you brought her out here, so I can tell you if the chic is lying or not, but I gotta hear it from you now."

"Hear what?" I ask.

He jabs his finger in my chest. "Your version of the story."

I rub the back of my neck where the tension has been building over the past few weeks, then proceed to tell him how I originally met Mickey and everything else leading up to this very moment. Even as I retell it, I find myself running through various stages of anger. By the time I'm done, my knuckles are tight on the back of the chair and wait for Gutter to weigh in on what I've just said.

Gutter isn't one for speaking without thinking. It's one of the things I've always liked about him. When I'm done, he doesn't launch into anything. He simply sits in silence, allowing my words to sink into his brain.

The song of a million crickets grows louder in the quiet until it's humming so loud I can feel it vibrating against my skin.

Finally, Gutter speaks. "My question for you is what are you hoping to learn from bringing her here?"

Before Gutter was, well, Gutter, he was Christopher Andrews, a phycologist in the military. He spent his time studying how the mind is affected by torture and deciding which techniques worked best and which didn't work at all. He was good, too. They used to call him the human lie detector. Not because he could necessarily tell you if the person was lying or not, but because he knew exactly what means to use to extract the truth.

Needless to say that lying to Gutter is pointless, so I never have. "I just need to know if I'm wasting my time with her. If she's ever going to tell me what I need to know"

"You said she suffered a head injury. How?" Gutter asks.

I recall the moment right before I found out that Mickey was a she and not a he.

"By way of headbutt," I answer. "After that, she seemed confused for a little while. When I first met her she was the same way. Thinking people were around her who weren't there. Don't know what happened to her that night though. She says a kayaking or swimming accident or some shit, but I don't fucking know."

"What do you know?" Gutter asks.

I feel like I don't know shit anymore for certain except for two things. I need the information only she knows, and I want to fuck her more than I want to breathe.

I tell Gutter neither of those things. Although from the amused look on his face, he already knows.

Gutter scratches his whiskers. "Well, for what it's worth, I think she's telling the truth." He retrieves two more beers and passes one to me. "What she told me, anyway. But I can sense that her intentions aren't in line with the intentions of whoever she's working for. That girl has got her own agenda, so you may want to find out what that is if you have any hope of cracking her."

Gutter's right. If she has reasons of her own behind her actions, then I can use those reasons to get her to give me the information I need.

He raises an eyebrow at me. "You was hoping she was lying to you?"

"I was hoping you would tell me to take a knife to her flesh, or remove her fingernails, and she'd tell me everything." I press the cold bottle to my forehead to alleviate the budding headache threatening to burst through my skull.

"Nope. She's what I would call a resistor. Her will is too strong for any of the usual antics. Like I said, find out *her* truth, and you'll find out *the* truth." Gutter leans his elbows on his thighs. "I'll tell you one thing: You can't keep the girl locked up. That ain't going to help shit. Not with a girl like that. If anything, it will make her more determined to keep her mouth shut."

"Why is that?" I press.

"Simple. If she hates you, she ain't gonna open up to you. You've got to gain her trust. Get her to make the decision on her own. Let her know that her world ain't gonna implode if she unburdens herself by telling you her secrets."

I blow out a breath and crack my neck. "I don't think I've got that kind of time. Or if it's possible at this point." I think back to what I've subjected her to and don't see how she's going to trust me after that or how she won't see right through the act.

Gutter smiles. "She's smart. She ain't gonna fall for your tactics because she'll know they're tactics. I've told her about your kindness, and I've opened up the door. You've just gotta suck up your pride and walk through it. Be as real as you can. It's not hard to be kind to her. She's a good soul. Reminds me of my Atty." Gutter looks to the sky with a sad smile.

"You sure a knife to her flesh won't work?" I groan.

"Is a ten-pound rabbit a big rabbit?" he counters.

I don't know much about rabbits and have no idea if a ten-pound rabbit is, in fact, a big rabbit. "I sure as shit hope so."

"You got feelings for this girl or something?" he suddenly asks.

I laugh. "I got feelings for her all right. None of them good." I stand and toss an empty beer bottle into the bucket that doubles as a trash can. I head to the door to retrieve Mickey.

"Pike," Gutter calls out.

I glance over my shoulder. Gutter stands and places his thumbs under his suspenders again, rocking back on the heels of his plastic boots. "What happens to the girl after you find out the truth?"

"That depends on what the truth is."

Gutter frowns. His voice is calm if not slightly sad. "Be careful, Pike. They say the truth hurts for a fucking reason."

That is something I already know all too well.

Pushing open the doors, I glance around the houseboat. What I find makes my anger flare and a roar tear from my throat.

Because what I find is nothing.

Mickey's gone.

CHAPTER SIXTEEN
MICKEY

INSIDE GUTTER'S HOUSEBOAT IS ONE SINGLE ROOM SURROUNDED BY accordion metal walls. The kitchen consists of a rusted utility sink, a portable electric burner set on top of a crate, and the cooler he told me I'd find inside. A cot sits in the corner, with mesh netting hanging from the ceiling above.

I'm suddenly too aware of being alone although Gutter and Pike are talking only a few feet away. It feels wrong as it often does, especially since growing up with three sisters I was very rarely alone. The past five days have been a lesson in being alone as well as a test of how much I can…wait.

Any captive held longer than a period of one week must be either killed when the clock strikes midnight on the fifth day…

It's one of the guidelines on the ridiculous memo I found in Pike's truck. At least, I thought it was ridiculous until I just realized that today is day five.

If Pike is planning on following those guidelines, it means I'm almost out of time.

I push aside my panic, searching for logic amongst the fear.

I know what I need to do.

No, what I *have* to do.

I risk a glance through a crack in the door. Pike and Gutter are deep in conversation. Good. It'll buy me time.

I move quickly and quietly. While my brain is screaming for me to hurry, I take it as slow as I possibly can, padding to the back of the room. At a pace slower than a snail's I push aside one of the metal panels in the back of the room. The murky water below looks like a vat of tar.

Don't think about it. Just do it.

With a deep breath, I crouch down on the wooden planks, then slowly lower myself into the water so as not to make even the slightest ripple. It's over eighty degrees outside, but the water might as well be from the arctic. It's that cold. My teeth chatter as I begin to move, walking slowly through the waist deep water, too slowly for the pace my mind is racing and heart is beating. It's not until I'm deep enough inside the reeds to be hidden from view that I pick up my pace. Thankfully the black water is shallower here, hitting at my knees. But it's also thick and filled with grass and weeds and I don't want to know what else. My thighs burn with the effort it takes to lift my feet from the mud that sucks them in with each step. I walk for what seems like hours, but in reality I have no idea how long it's been. I keep my eyes trained straight ahead into the dark to avoid spotting whatever critters might be lurking nearby.

What you don't know can't hurt you. It doesn't exactly apply in this situation because I'm pretty sure an alligator I don't know is there can hurt me, but I'm going to go with it and pretend it makes sense.

A sigh of relief escapes me as I reach an area surrounded by cypress trees where the water is only ankle deep. My jeans are soaked through, wet and heavy against my skin. I slap a mosquito on my cheek, shaking off the dead, bloody bug from my palm. The hot night air feels icy as it blows over my wet skin. I shiver, rubbing my hands over my arms.

A honk of a horn in the distance drags my attention toward

an embankment up ahead. As quickly as I can, I trudge toward the sound. When I don't hear it again, I think I imagined it.

But I see lights. Headlights.

My shoes get sucked into the mud, falling free from my feet, but soon, my foot lands on more solid soil. My feet ache and sting as I step on countless sharp branches and rocks. It takes everything I have left to climb the embankment.

My hair snags on a branch. Untangling it would take time I don't have, so I use my hand and yank, pulling it free from the tree and some of it free from my head.

When my feet hit pavement, I know I've found the road.

Minutes pass without another car, and I remember that I'm in the middle of nowhere in the Everglades. The chances of spotting another car out here in the middle of the night are slim to none.

With nothing to do but wait, I begin walking toward where I think the highway could be. A wild boar runs across the road a few feet in front of me, and I cover my mouth to keep from shrieking and drawing attention to myself.

Headlights appear behind me. I turn around, happy to see it's a car and not Pike's truck. I leap into the middle of the road, waving and jumping around frantically until it slows to a stop.

I round the car, an older style classic black Cadillac. I reach the driver's side window just as it rolls down.

"Thank you so much for stopping," I say, not realizing how out of breath I am until I have to stop to breathe for a second so I can continue. "I've been kidnapped. I need to go to the police. Or anywhere where there's people. A gas station if the police station is too far."

I couldn't actually walk into a police station, but asking for a ride to where I really need to go would draw questions I'm not going to answer. More than anything I just need to get into town.

The man cocks his head and looks me over, revealing a

tangle of vine tattoos on each side of his head. "Who kidnapped you?" He takes a drag on his cigarette, and I quickly realize from the smell that it's not tobacco he's smoking.

"His name is Pike. I've been locked in his apartment. He took me out here to meet someone, and I escaped through the swamp."

"So that's what that smell is…" he says, taking in my mud-covered state. "Okay, okay, hop in. I'll give you a ride to the Logan's Beach police station. I'm heading in that direction anyway." He reaches over to the passenger side and opens the door.

I blow out a breath of relief and round the car. I jump in and slam the door shut.

"Are you hurt?" the man asks, putting the car in drive. His dress shirt is rolled up to his elbows exposing his tattooed forearms as he fiddles with the radio station.

I shake my head. "No. I mean, I don't think so. Just a little banged up."

"So, this Pike fellow, he's a gentle kidnapper then?"

We pass under a street light, and I notice the man's yellow bow-tie and matching suspenders. *Street light. We're getting closer to civilization.*

I remember his earlier question. "Are there different levels of being held against your will?"

He nods. "Several."

Now, I'm curious. "How would you know?"

He smiles and bobs his head to the Taylor Swift song playing on the radio. "Just trust me, I know every level of kidnapping and torture there is to know. Been there. Done that. Burned the motherfucking t-shirt." He turns onto a road next to the highway, and I almost cry out for joy when we spot a sign that says *Welcome to Logan's Beach.*

"What's your name?" he asks.

I rub my hands over my arms, feeling cold even in the heat

as the water dries on my skin. "Michaela, but they call me Mickey."

He pulls one hand off the wheel and extends it to me. "I'm—"

The phone I was about to ask him if I can use rings. He answers before it can do so a second time. "Hey, Doc. What's cracka-lackin'?" There's a small pause. His eyes go wide. "He did what? Again?" he says, trying to fight a smile. "It's my wife," he explains.

Another pause. "Oh, that's just Mickey. She was kidnapped. Found her on the side of the road. I'm just giving her a ride. Very magnanimous of me, I know. But, back to Bo."

His wife doesn't seem to mind what he's just said or at the very least isn't surprised because his response tells me that they have, in fact, gone back to the prior conversation.

"I don't understand the problem. I wrote a letter to his principal explaining everything. Isn't that what parents do? Write letters explaining their child's slightly off-colored borderline homicidal behavior?" he says, tapping his fingers on the wheel.

He blows out a breath. "What do you mean there's no such thing as an emotional support knife?"

Pause.

"Isn't there a dog we can get him? Like a homicide dog?"

Pause.

"No, I was not aware that's not what a homicide dog does. But you gotta admit, it would be cool if they did." He chuckles.

We turn down another street, and the lights of town appear in the distance.

"Fine, we will talk about it tonight after the sex but before the weapons sweep," he relents, hanging up the phone.

"You got kids?" he asks, lighting another joint.

"Not that I know of," I reply, feeling the best I have in days, knowing that I'm free.

He bobs his head to the music again. "Kidnapped and still

got jokes? Wow, we have a lot more in common than I thought. All things considered."

"All things considered?" I question.

I look outside and recognize the street. I spot Pike's Pawn up ahead, and dread fills my stomach.

Stop worrying. You're free now. It's on the main road. We have to pass it to get anywhere in this town.

The car begins to slow. He parks it at the curb outside the pawn shop.

My chest tightens with panic. "Why are we stopping here?" I ask, turning sideways toward him in my seat.

"Never abandon your captive," he says, and immediately, I recognize those words.

I don't reply because the passenger door is ripped open, and I'm pulled from my seat by a strong set of arms. "Noooo!" I scream.

"Hello, again, Mic." I look up into familiar dark eyes, burning with rage and something more sadistic.

My skin both heats and crawls.

I look back to the man. One last silent plea for help. One glance tells me that help won't come. I don't know the man, yet his betrayal stings, leaving me feeling vulnerable and exposed. *Why?* I silently ask.

He grins as if he's an Uber driver hoping for a decent rating. "Because we don't betray our own here," he answers, as if the answer is that simple to him. "Besides, just like my son, Bo, Pike's not so bad once you get past all the scary shit." He thinks for a minute. "If you can get past the scary shit." He puts the car in drive. "By the way, I'm Samuel Clearwater. My friends call me Preppy."

Preppy drives off with a wave. "You two kids have fun!"

Fun. Yeah right. There's so many possibilities of what will happen now, but fun most certainly isn't one of them.

Pike cradles my face in his big rough hands, forcing me to

stare up at him. The metal of the handcuffs are cold and rough against my cheeks. "What to do with you now?" he asks, searching my eyes. It's not his usual warning. I get the feeling he's not asking me, but posing the question to himself.

Pike slowly walks me backward, hands still on my face, until I'm pressed against the base of one of the large palm trees lining the road.

Preppy is wrong. There will be no getting past the scary shit. Not with Pike. Not now.

Not ever.

But I've dealt with my fair share of scary men, and I remind myself that I'm not the frightened girl I once was. I'm strong and capable.

Before I can complete the thought, I act, landing my fist below his ribs. My hand stings. "Bitch," he breathes, nostrils flaring as he looks down at where my fist is balled.

He wasn't expecting my punch, so I figure the next will come as even more of a surprise. I swing my left arm up, connecting with the underside of his elbow. His hand falls from my face. Rearing back my head and gritting my teeth, I take a page out of Pike's book and go for the headbutt. Only, Pike is so much taller than me. I only manage to connect with his chin and cause my vision to momentarily blur.

"Fuck," he curses, rubbing his chin.

I duck under his arm and make a run for it. The shell road slicing into my already injured feet. I only manage to make it a few steps before his massive body collides with my back, sending me crashing onto the ground.

I gasp for breath as the wind is knocked out of me. "Still got some fight in you, Mic. We'll see what we can do to change that." His breath is low in my ear as my cheek is pressed into the sharp shell.

He raises off me, and I'm finally able to take a full breath.

He flips me over, trapping my wrists above my head. His hair falls into his eyes as his gaze drinks me in.

The chill in the air heats. The hairs on my arm stand on end as we stare at one another without saying a word.

Thick silence fills the space between us. The only sound is heavy breathing and my own thudding heartbeat. I count them to measure the time. Ba-boom. One. Ba-boom. Two.

Pike's dark eyes are pinning me to the ground as much as his hands on my wrists.

Ba-boom. Three.

And then his lips are on mine.

I push back on his chest only to realize I've got a fistful of his shirt, and I'm not pushing, but pulling him against me. His lips on mine feel like I think

Evidence of his arousal strains against his jeans, I gasp as it juts against my thigh.

"I told you I like it when you fight back," he groans against my lips.

He's so fucking arrogant and so cocky and his lips are heaven and hell. I bite at his lip, drawing blood only to be rewarded with a bite of his own. He rises up and swipes at the red smear on my lip with his thumb, sucking it into his mouth.

He lifts me from the ground so that I'm straddling his lap on the curb. I slap his face so hard my palm stings. His eyes darken, and I realize too late that was the wrong thing to do. He wraps his hand around my throat, squeezing, but not hard enough for me not to be able to breath. His lips are on mine again, and I hate that I moan when his tongue pushes past the seam of my lips and our tongues war with one another. He threads his other hand through my hair, yanking hard. I grab his hair with both hands and do the same. He hisses then grins. It continues like this. An endless cycle of punishment and pleasure.

His hand digs into my upper thigh, before unbuttoning my

jeans. He snakes his hand inside, and it's so fucking wrong but so right. I'm wet for him, yearning for him to touch me there. His rough hand on my skin has me shaking with anticipation as his fingers descend lower and lower. His lips suck and bite at my neck. The pleasure courses through me, and I moan loud into his ear. His finger reaches my clit, barely brushing it, but the shock and pleasure has me writhing on his lap.

"Pike!" Thorne's shout is an ice bucket, pouring cold reality on top of our heads, dousing the lust fueled flames.

Flames that should never have been burning in the first place.

CHAPTER SEVENTEEN
MICKEY

"Pike!" Thorne's voice calls out again.

Pike stands, tossing me off his lap. He looks calm and put together as he lights a cigarette. The only evidence of what we just did is the large bulge straining the front of his pants.

I, on the other hand, look as if I'd just swam through a swamp. Which I did.

We're in the shadows, and I'm pretty sure Thorne can't see us from where she is, but I'm even more sure that Pike doesn't want her to see us because he steps in front of me, blocking me from view.

"Meet me by the garage. Quick!" she adds, disappearing around the building. Pike takes my hand in his and drags me in her direction. I still taste his lips on mine and feel dizzy from it all, but he looks as collected and as angry as ever.

I'm thankful for the interruption. A chance to collect my thoughts. To become logical me instead of reckless me.

Pike turns around. Again, his face is cold and impassive. "This changes nothing," he remarks flatly.

His words sting, and I know what he said, but then why do I hear something else? Something underneath his coldness. As if what he really said was *This changes everything.*

Pike grabs on my hand, tugging me out of the shadows and into the parking lot.

Thorne gives me a once over, popping her gun. "What the fuck happened to you?"

"The swamp happened to me," I reply.

She shrugs, and like she's told me before, she doesn't ask questions.

"What the fuck do you want to show me? I've got something I've got to take care of," Pike spits, sparing me a glance.

Me. He's got to take care of me. And not in the bubble bath and foot rub kind of way.

Thorne leans down and yanks open the garage bay. Inside is a large white truck with no markings. I recognize it instantly as the truck I'd helped steal from Pike. There was no mention of bringing it back. It makes no sense that it would be here at all.

What the fuck is going on? Whatever part of the plan this is, I wasn't there when it was discussed because even I don't understand the motives behind going through all the trouble to steal something like this, only to bring it back.

Pike takes a step forward as if he can't believe what he's seeing.

"Can you believe it?" Thorne asks, smiling from ear to ear.

"How?" Pike asks, pressing his palm to the bumper and pulling himself inside the open gate. There are barrels of hazardous waste lining both sides of the truck. He opens a few to check the contents.

He looks to me and repeats the question. "How?"

"The honest to God truth is that I have no idea," I reply. "I'm just as confused as you are."

Thorne shrugs. "I have no idea either. I came out to store a Vespa, and when I opened the bay, boom, it was back." She makes a mind-blown gesture with her hands.

The sound of a motorcycle pulling into the parking lot

vibrates through the garage, the echo growing so loud I cover my ears until a shiny black bike pulls up and cuts the engine.

The man is huge and dressed in all black. There are belts wrapped around his muscular forearms. He stares up at the truck and then at Pike. His bright green eyes blazing with fury.

"What's going on?" I whisper to Thorne. Her eyes are wide and she presses a finger over her mouth, indicating that I should shut mine.

The man jerks his chin to the truck. "Care to explain why I got a mysterious phone call suggesting I should check your fucking garage and how when I do I find you standin' out here with the truck that you told me got jacked?" He turns suspicious green eyes on Pike. "We need to fucking talk."

☙

Thorne leads me back to Pike's room and makes sure I again have everything I need for a shower. When I ask her who the man in the garage is, she simply says, "King."

I know the name. I've heard it before, but never in a context that would give me enough info to classify him as enemy or friend or associate.

I wrap a towel around my body and sit at the edge of the bed. There's a laptop open on the dresser. I walk over to it, and press a key. The screen comes to life. It's not password protected. "Idiot," I mutter. The screen has several squares of black and white videos. The upper right-hand corner is the garage. I rewind it until I see familiar men in skull masks pulling the truck in before racing into an awaiting van and speeding off.

I fast forward it to now, when King and Pike are deep in conversation. I wish the video had sound so I can hear what they're discussing. But something else draws my attention inside the open truck gate. I zoom in on the contents and compare it with the memory of the night we'd taken it, searching for a difference I know is there.

The locks clicks open. Instinctively, I tighten the towel around my body. Pike stalks in and notices what I've been watching. "Care to explain?" he asks.

"I wish I could," I answer honestly.

"You need to explain, or this isn't going to end fucking well for you," Pike grates. It's not quite a warning, but an explanation, a plea for the truth I can never give him. "This isn't a fucking game, Mic, and I'm done fucking playing. Talk now."

"You...you'd kill me," I reply. It's not a question.

"Mic, I'm running out of fucking patience, and yes, I'd kill anyone who crosses me. I don't discriminate. Not only did your buddies steal from me, but they returned my shit to frame me and make it look like I was trying to keep all the profits for myself. Whoever is behind this is out to fucking destroy my life. Everything I've worked for. I had to talk King off a fucking ledge, and he's still not satisfied with my answer of I don't know how the fuck it got here or why the fuck it's back."

I don't know what to tell him that could take the pain and anger from his face and not destroy everything I've been working so hard for. I take a deep breath. "It's the fifth day. What are you going to do?"

He eyes me suspiciously. "Jesus Christ! I'm not following those fucking rules. I'm just trying to protect what's mine and hurt the people who are fucking hurting my business. My friends." He stares at me; his eyes are daggers being thrown into my heart. "But you wouldn't know about protecting people. You're too selfish and caught up in some bullshit you think is more important. You may be smart, but you're also fucking selfish."

His words cut a cavern within my chest. An empty place once only filled with hate and sorrow not an expanse of pain. Because he isn't wrong, but he also isn't right. "You're right. My intentions are selfish. But don't think for one fucking second that you own the rights on protecting those you love because you don't know shit about what I've been through or why I do what I do."

"Because you won't fucking tell me!" he screams.

Pike stalks over to me and grabs me by the throat. A sharp pang of fear expands in my chest. I glance around for a weapon but only find the computer screen. Suddenly, what I was looking for earlier becomes obvious. "Wait!" I cry, pushing against his chest. "The barrels. They have white packaging with a piece of black tape over the top."

"And?" he says, slowly releasing his hold on me, blinking away the anger possessing him.

I point to the screen. "Look. In the video, they have the same tape, but it's thicker than I saw it downstairs, and it's wrapped differently. There are two passes over the packages instead of one."

"They've been tampered with," he says, staring at the screen.

"That's what I'm thinking." Keeping my towel tight around my body. "Do you have a pen and paper?"

"Why?"

"Because there are some things we'll need if you want to know for sure."

⚬

After I write down what I'll need, Pike storms out. I take the opportunity to get dressed in one of Pike's t-shirts I find in the dresser since I don't want to put the muddy ones back on. I comb through my wet hair and brush my teeth. I check the alarm clock on the nightstand. He's been gone for over an hour, and I'm beginning to think he's not coming back and has blown off my idea as another tactic of manipulation.

After almost two hours, the door opens. Pike enters with one of the packages from the truck and a crate containing plastic jugs of the chemicals I requested. I'm not going to ask him how he managed to get them since the only place I know of that would have them on hand are labs and industrial chemical plants.

"The kitchen will be easier," I suggest. "More space."

He motions for me to follow him. He sets everything down on the counter, and I go to work setting out what I'll need, making sure to identify each liquid individually and placing them in a line in the order I'll be using them. "You have a clean bowl? Glass would be preferred."

He opens the cabinets and pulls out a brandy glass, setting it on the counter beside my elbow. "This will work."

Pike takes a seat at the counter on one of the stools and watches as I work, delicately combining a fragile mix of chemicals that, if not handled properly, could blow this place to smithereens.

He shakes his head as if he can't believe he agreed to this. "You could be building a fucking bomb for all I know."

I shake my head and swirl the contents of the glass. "Nope, but it could do some damage in untrained hands," I offer. "A bomb would require a current. A car battery or…" I notice Pike staring at me. It's probably best not to explain to him how to build a bomb, never mind let him know I can build one with household items. A powerful one, too. "Uh, never mind."

I glance to the plastic package. "Open it," I instruct him.

Pike unsheathes his knife and is about to cut into the package.

I hold out my hand to stop him.

"What now?" he barks.

I smile flatly. "Wash it first."

He rises to his feet and washes the knife in the sink with soap and water. The counter space is limited, his bicep brushing my forearm as he dries the now gleaming knife. The electric current I felt outside hums between us once again. My skin becomes all too aware of his presence, and I squeeze my legs together to stop the pulsing of unmet need pounding there.

I let out a held breath when he rounds the counter and again perches on his stool, putting some much-needed distance between us.

He stabs a hole into the package. "How many do you need?"

"Just one," I reply. "Drop it into the glass."

He scoops one pill from the package and hovers the knife above the glass. "Slowly" I say, crouching down so that I'm eye level with the glass. I raise my palm. "Very slowly."

Pike lowers the blade inside the glass without touching the liquid. He slowly flips it, dropping the white pill into the clear thick liquid. "What now?" he asks, sheathing his knife in his boot.

"Now, we wait." I lift the glass, slowly swirling the contents. "It should only be a few…" The liquid begins to change to a light blue, and after a few seconds, it's much darker, the color of the stuff used to unclog drains, confirming my suspicions.

I set the glass down carefully.

Pike leans over the counter, staring down into the glass. "Well?"

I point to the glass. "It's definitely been tampered with. The MDMA has been laced with fentanyl and judging by the color…" I tap the rim. "This one pill contains a ton of it. If it were ingested…" I pause unable to process how someone could target innocent kids looking to have a good time, regardless of the reason behind it.

"What?" Pike asks, slapping his hands down on the counter.

I jump. "It would be lethal."

Pike picks up the glass.

"What are you doing?" I ask, curiously.

He doesn't answer. Instead, Pike takes the entire glass in his hand and looks at the color as if he can't believe what he's seeing. Then, with an angry roar he throws the glass over my head and it shatters against the cabinets. I crouch down behind the cabinet, a failed attempt to hide from his wrath.

"Go to sleep," he orders.

"You...you're not?" I ask, not knowing how to finish my sentence because I don't really know what I'm asking. *You're not going to murder me right now?* Seemed too much like a reminder to keep him on task.

He balls up his fists. His chest is heaving. He leans his head against the wall and punches it with his fist. "Not tonight. Tonight, I have other shit I've got to deal with."

I feel a strong need to comfort him, which is strange under the circumstances.

"Go to bed," he orders again. He steps outside of the room. The locks click in place. I hear him talking on the phone, his voice fading as he moves down the stairs.

Bed? How can I sleep now? After all that's happened? But the thought of how much I can't sleep or just sleep at all makes me yawn, and I realize that I'm tired. Mentally. Physically.

My mind goes back to the kiss.

Emotionally.

I pad over to the bed and pull the covers back, plopping in with zero grace. I lift the blanket over my chest. Sleep doesn't come. I lay there for hours running every scenario I can think of regarding where we go from here. None of them ends with me making it through this alive except alien invasion where the aliens accidentally drop me from their laser beam pulling me into their ship and I fall into a soft pile of hay.

The lock clicks open and the door shuts softly and clicks back into place. I hear Pike thud over to the bed and kick off his boots, tossing his shirt to the floor, followed by the unmistakable sound of his belt and then his jeans hitting the floor before.

I feel the dipping of the mattress beside me.

"You're going to sleep here?" I whisper, pulling the blanket tighter over my chest.

"Do you see another bed?" he asks.

"No," I say.

"Go to sleep, Mic. There'll be plenty of time to argue and want to kill each other tomorrow. Tonight, you did something good. The bad shit that comes along with it will still be here to worry about when the suns up."

"What did I do that was good, again?" I ask, needing to know what he's referring to.

He sighs. "You pointed out that the packages had been tampered with, and that there was enough fentanyl in those pills that it would have killed the stupid kids who take it." I feel the tension in his body from across the bed. "My question is why? Why tell me at all? Why not just let it happen?"

"That wasn't something good. I just don't want innocent people to die," I say simply. "I don't want anyone to die."

"But, why go against your own people? They're plans?"

Now it's my turn to sigh. "I can only tell you that every decision I make is for no one but myself and my own conscience, and I'm honestly sorry that this is hurting you." My chest tightens.

"What game are you playing at, Mic?" he asks, calmly. Too calm.

I chuckle. "Playing insinuates that I might lose. I'm not playing at any game because losing isn't an option."

"You don't belong in that world," he says, sounding every bit sincere. "Or this one. You just don't."

"No, I don't," I admit, and it's the truth. I don't belong in that world.

But when all of this is over, that world will belong to *me*.

CHAPTER EIGHTEEN
PIKE

THE MEETING WITH KING AND NINE HAD BEEN BRUTAL. Although, King now understands that I'm not trying to cut him out by pretending to steal my own shipment that he funded. The worst part is, Nine vouched for me. If King continued to believe that I wasn't to be trusted, ultimately, it would be Nine who could pay. I can't have that happening to my friend, certainly not because of me.

But it's not going to happen. Because of *her*.

I stare down at Mickey, fast asleep, her little purring snore the only sound in the otherwise quiet room.

I want to wrap my hands around her beautiful throat and choke the intel from her perfect mouth, but Gutter is right. The girl is stronger and physical violence would cause her not to trust me and I need her to trust me if I'm going to get what I need.

I cringe at the look in her eyes when I told her after the kiss that this changes nothing. It was a lie. It changes everything. Once I tasted her, I couldn't stop tasting her. Covered in mud or not, I can't lie to myself and pretend I wasn't ready to take her right there on the curb.

Stupid fucking move on my part. Giving into my primal

urge to kiss her, to claim her, then dismissing her right after we were interrupted isn't going to open the doors to honesty.

I brush her hair from her eyes and can't help but smile when she makes a noise of protest and moves her head so that she's face-down in the pillow.

The way she used her photographic memory and her impressive big brain even after I'd treated her so coldly to alert me to the tampering. Only to ruin plans her own people obviously had to destroy my reputation and my connection with King. She helped me.

No, I remind myself. I can't think like that. She did it to save people, not me. And yet, that doesn't make me feel any less of an asshole for the way I've been treating her. The thing is, looking back on my life, I can't remember a time when I've ever felt guilty for being an asshole. There isn't a thing in my life I can say that I regret saying or doing even if those actions resulted in hurting other people either physically or emotionally.

She's not the selfish person I accused her of being. Selfish people don't save the lives of thousands of unaware ravers hellbent on a good time. They don't thwart their own people in the name of others.

But Mickey did.

Which leads me to believe that Gutter's right in yet another way. She has her own agenda. She's pretty much told me that herself. She might not be able tell me who is behind all of this, but if what Gutter said is right and I can get her to tell me what it is, then it could give me enough to lead me straight to the motherfucker's door.

My eyes sting with exhaustion.

I can't sleep. Not just because of all the shit that's gone down over the past few days, but because of her.

My cock stiffens at the thought of Mickey in my bed. Of

knowing she's within arm's reach and that she's only wearing one of my t-shirts.

Fuck this. I get out of bed, head to the bathroom and start the shower, turning the dial to cold. I step under the spray, but even the icy blast isn't enough to douse the burning need throbbing in my cock.

Facing the tile, I take my cock in hand. Taking a deep breath, I allow my thoughts to run free. I think of the way Mickey responded to my kiss. Her innocence shown in the way she didn't quite know how to kiss me back, but did it anyway because she wanted to. Everything I gave her in that kiss she gave right fucking back to me. All while we were both fighting against this weird thing pulling us together. The fucking want in her eyes. The way her body responded to mine. Her little moans and gasps. If Thorne hadn't interrupted us I know I could've made her come right there on the fucking curb. The way she rode me, seeking her own pleasure, knowing that I could be the one to give it to her.

It doesn't take long until my balls draw up tight and I'm coming in long hard bursts, streaming days of pent up desire all over the yellow tile. After I catch my breath, I turn the spray to rinse off the wall. I lather up, rinse off, and grab a towel hanging from a hook on the wall as I step out of the shower.

I dab at the water on my face and catch the scent of the cucumber girly shampoo Thorne gave to Mickey.

Instantly, I'm hard again.

I mentally swear, drying off as quickly as possible.

Clicking off the bathroom light, I pad back over to the bed and lift the blankets, the mattress dipping under my weight as I settle my head on the pillow. I turn my head and stare at the small shadowy lump underneath the blankets beside me.

Now more than ever, I realize that I want to know what makes Mickey tick.

I roll away from her to face the door. I close my eyes, but it doesn't close out the unwelcome thought that follows.

I don't want to get to know her for any admission of truth, but because I genuinely want to know everything there is to know about her.

I finally fall asleep only to have a dream I haven't had in years. But it isn't a dream at all.

It's a gut-punch of a fucking memory.

Five Years Old

"Hey, big boy. Come with me so we can talk for a minute, okay?" Mom looks at me, but her eyes don't look right. They're bloodshot and glassy with bags underneath. I've seen her upset before, many times, but never like this. Her hand is shaking and sweaty as she takes mine in hers, leading me into the small living room. She sits me down on the couch. Her hand never leaves mine. "Daddy's left us. For good this time."

She's waiting for a reaction that will never come. I never saw the man, and when I did, he was beating on my mother. Why is she so upset? People who aren't good in our lives shouldn't be in our lives. "The thing is I can't do this alone. I'm not... I can't...I just can't," she sobs. "I'm so sorry, baby. You deserve so much better."

I don't care what I deserve. I want her.

"I don't understand," I say, holding her hand tighter as she tries to pull away.

She looks at me for a few seconds before smiling sadly. She ruffles my hair. "Never mind. Mommy loves you. I will always love you. That's all you need to know. Everything will be fine. I promise."

She sniffles and wipes her tears away. She stands. "Do you want to watch a movie?"

I nod, convinced everything is going to be okay like she said because I'm five and she's my mom.

She disappears into the kitchen and a few minutes later comes back with a large bowl of popcorn, a bottle of water, and all of my favorite candy. She clicks the remote and presses play on my favorite superhero movie.

"Mommy has to take care of something. I'll be right back," she says. Or at least, that's what I think she says. I'm too engrossed in the opening battle scene playing before me to really listen. I don't even notice the door opening or closing or anything else for that matter because I fall asleep.

When I wake up from a junk-food induced coma, there's three men in uniforms staring down at me. Policemen. "You alone, kid?" they ask.

I look around. "My mommy is here. We were watching a movie. I fell asleep."

The officers exchange a knowing glance. "Ain't no one here, kid. Your mommy's the one who called us. Come on. You're going to come with us. It will all be okay."

I don't believe him, not like I believe my mom. She's coming back. She said she would come back.

"She's coming back!" I yell as they pick me up. I kick and cry out of their grasp. "She's coming back!"

One sighs loudly and sounds sadder than my mommy had sounded. "No, kid. She ain't coming back."

They lead me to the patrol car, and one gets in the backseat with me while the other two get into the front.

The last thing I remember seeing as we drive off is my mother hiding behind the trash cans in the alley next to our house. She's pressing her middle finger to her lips to silence me as tears run down her face.

I was sad but also angry. I turned away from her and looked at the back of the seat instead.

She said she loved me, but she left me.

If this is what love is, I want no part of it.

CHAPTER NINETEEN
MICKEY

THE NEXT MORNING PIKE DRAGS ME DOWN THE STAIRS INTO THE pawn shop before I'm fully awake. The showroom smells like silver polish and stale cigarettes. It's the first time I've been in it long enough to actually look around and take it in, but I can't because Pike plops me down in a chair next to the counter.

I dart my eyes from one side of the room to the other, waiting for the preverbal monster to jump out at me. "What's going on?"

Pike crouches in front of me. "Did I kill you yesterday?"

I cock my head and take a deep breath. Still alive. "No."

Pike grins. "The way I see it, you and me need to come to an understanding. You won't try and run off again, and I won't hurt you while I'm trying to figure shit out. There's no need for us to be down each other's throats all the fucking time. I got enough shit to worry about."

I'm hesitant to accept his offer of a truce, but my thought is interrupted when a pretty blonde girl not much older than myself walks through the door. She's wearing a pink shirt that reads, "Okay, Karen." Without greeting Pike, she begins removing tools from a blue tote bag she sets down at my feet.

Thorne steps into the room. "Pike, I need you," she says.

Pike rises to his feet. "Be right back."

He leaves me alone with the blonde girl who's humming to herself as she works.

"Who are you?" I ask.

She removes a small black box from her bag and presses a screwdriver into one of the holes until a black band connecting it is released on one side. "I'm Rage. I'll be your friendly house arrest bracelet installer today." She removes a pair of latex gloves from her back pocket and snaps them on. "Tell me, have you had any sneezing, coughing or fever in the last forty-eight hours?"

House arrest bracelet installer? He said he wasn't following the guidelines! "Uh, no."

"Good. Have you eaten anything from the bar next door or touched anything from said bar including, but not limited to: door handles, bar stools, restroom stall handles, etcetera?" She kneels at my feet and fixes the strap around my ankle. Again, she uses the screwdriver, but this time to click the band back into place.

I point to the device. "No, but what does any of that have to do with whatever it is that you're doing?"

Rage shakes her head, whipping her blond ponytail into and out of her face. "Nothing. I just don't want to catch the plague while installing this beautiful work of art, and the bar next door looks like a fucking cesspool." She cringes.

"What exactly does this thing do?" I ask, having never had to wear a house arrest bracelet. Rage twists the screwdriver once more and stands to admire her handiwork.

"It's a bomb," she says, casually, confirming my suspicions. "There. All done."

"I'm sorry, it's a what?" I ask, white knuckling the chair.

Rage looks up at me and tilts her head. "You know…a bomb? Bombs go boom?" She makes an exploding motion with her hands. "Why do people never seem to understand what a bomb is? What are they teaching in school these days?"

"Not how to install bombs on people!" I learned all my bomb knowledge long after I was done with school.

She shrugs. "Shame."

I try to collect my thoughts. "I know what a bomb is. I just want to know why this one is strapped to my ankle."

She rolls her eyes. "Because it would look tacky on your wrist."

"She giving you trouble?" Pike asks. He moves from behind me to stand next to Rage.

"No, but she doesn't know what a bomb is," Rage mutters. "You sure know how to pick them, Pike."

He doesn't argue with her. Doesn't tell her that he didn't pick me and that I'm being held against my will, but I don't think Rage would be surprised...or care since she just strapped an explosive to my fucking body.

I glare at Pike. "Everything's honkey-dory here, Pike. Just us girls having a mani-pedi bomb installation session."

"Ugh, as if," Rage says, her nose wrinkles in disgust. "Do you know what kind of bacteria can be found on the tools of nail salons?" She tucks her screwdriver into a blue tote bag with a megaphone on the side. "Okay, that's it for me. Pike, I'll send you my bill. If you don't pay, I'll send you in pieces to your friends in the mail."

"How's Nolan these days?" Pike asks.

She sighs dreamily. "A model of the perfect non-murdering civilian as always," she replies. She picks up her tote bag and spares me one last glance, then looks to Pike, jerking her chin in my direction. "Teach the girl what a bomb is, will ya?"

The bell above the door rings, announcing her exit.

"I know what a bomb is," I mutter. Through the glass, I see Rage ride away on a baby blue Vespa. She peels out of the parking lot, kicking up gravel in her wake.

"You said you weren't following those stupid guidelines," I accuse.

"If I was following them, you'd be dead already," he points out. He isn't wrong. It's day six, by my count.

Pike stands before me and bends at the waist, placing his hands next to me on the arm rests of the chair. "We both know that you already know what a bomb is, so we're on the same page there. What I do have to explain is that if you go further than the parking lot or back alley, you'll get a warning beep. After that, you have ten-seconds to get back to where you need to be before it goes off. The same thing goes with tampering with it, except you'll get no warning."

Pike heads into the back room.

With my newfound freedom, I should go outside and breathe in some fresh air, but instead, I find myself following Pike. When I find him, he's bent over some kind of ledger, and to my surprise, there's a pair of black reading glasses perched on his nose. "Why did you take me to see Gutter the other day?"

"I told you. I needed to talk with him."

"You mean you needed to give him money?"

That gets his attention. He glances up at me. "He told you that?"

"Amongst other things, but what he didn't tell me is why you took me there. You could have left me tied to something. You didn't really have to bring me at all."

Pike closes the book and heads for the parking lot. "Remember, if it beeps, you've been warned."

I stomp my foot on the ground. "Arrogant child," I mutter under my breath.

"Because he wanted to know the truth," Thorne says, making her presence known. She's bent over in the corner, taking pictures of a china set. "To post in the online store," she explains when she sees me staring.

"What do you mean *because he wanted to know the truth*?" I ask, perching on a stool.

"Gutter is an enigma. One of those savants or whatever you call them." She arranges one of the delicate blue teacups to hide a chip in the corner then snaps a few shots, checking the screen on her camera after each one. "He can see your cracks when other people can't. That's why Pike took you there."

"He's a genius?" I nearly fall off my stool. "I wouldn't have guessed that."

"No one would."

"I like Gutter," I admit. "Now, I feel like I judged him too quickly, and I don't want to ever be that person. One who puts someone in a box they don't belong in."

Thorne removes the tea set from the backdrop, carefully wrapping each one in newspaper before delicately placing it back in a box with clothe dividers for each piece. "Can you grab me that violin?"

I slide off the stool and spot a violin case on a nearby table. I unlatch it and carefully pull it from the blue velvet lining. She places the box with the tea set on the shelf above her desk and holds out her hand for the violin. I hand it over and she again begins to meticulously arrange it in front of the bright green backdrop. "Don't be too hard on yourself for judging him. Gutter belongs in the box. In fact, he put himself in that box." She looks up from the camera. "No, scratch that. He built the fucking box."

Thorne laughs and takes another photo. She looks at the screen on the camera then turns to me. "He's not a technical genius by any stretch of the imagination, but he does have a superhuman ability. He even had a contract with the military as a torture specialist because of it."

Torture specialist?

I'm now wondering if the sensory torture wasn't entirely Pike's idea.

I watch Thorne work, fascinated by how careful she is with each piece as if it was something handed down to her by a beloved relative and near and dear to her heart.

"What exactly is this ability that makes him a good candidate as a specialist in torture?" I ask, puzzled.

Thorne snaps away, contorting her body into several different positions until she's finally satisfied with the shot. "Gutter was known in his day as the human lie detector."

"I told him everything," I say. "Well, *almost* everything."

"I know. He told Pike that you're telling the truth as you see it, which isn't the same as the truth. But also that you're hiding something. A secret that might not be yours to tell."

"He's not wrong," I say, wrapping my arms over my midsection.

Thorne points to the new accessory on my ankle. "For right now? For you?" She smiles. "It means you've leveled up."

I tilt my head. "Thorne, it's a *bomb*." I raise my foot and slap my heel down on the table. "On. My. Body." I pull it down. "What, exactly, have I leveled up to?"

She holds up two fingers. "Captive. Level two."

PIKE

Mickey looks around the pawn shop like she's taking a mental inventory. "Trying to figure out what else you can steal?" I ask. It's meant to be a tease but comes out harsher than I wanted. So far, this gaining her trust thing is going swell.

Her back jumps. I grin, taking great pleasure in being able to startle her so easily.

She runs her hands down the spine of a cello propped up on a stand at the end of one of the aisles. "No, I'm still trying to figure out something else. "

"And what, exactly, would that be?" I step down the aisle and meet her at the end.

"Who you really are. Sure, I picked up on some things in your apartment, but you're right, those were the obvious things. Stuff you don't try to hide." She plucks at one of the cello strings. "I've realized that I don't want to be quick to judge someone because people are a lot more complicated than they appear. Even you."

"Uh, thanks?" For a moment, I feel like I'm going to choke. "You don't have to try and analyze me. I'll tell you right now who I am. Someone you don't fuck with. That's all you need to know." I take a calming breath and try again. This time with less rage in my voice. "You already know enough," I say, sincerely.

She crosses her arms over her chest. The movement pushes up her tits and makes them jiggle, calling my attention to the perfectly round mounds peeking out from the neckline of her shirt. I'm beginning to recognize when the timid side of her shifts to the confident side. I enjoy that almost as much as startling her.

The tits thing ain't so bad either.

"I call bullshit," she replies.

I walk past her, brushing her shoulder. "Call it whatever you want. You know enough." I make a big fuss out of straightening the already straight cello as if she's knocked it to the ground. I glance at her over my shoulder. "You can try all you want, Mic." I stand again, looming over her. She doesn't waiver or back down. I rake my gaze over her mouth-watering tits and back up to her big grey eyes. She blushes and I lick my lips, liking how I can turn her face from pale white to pink with a simple look. "I'm not an experiment or a hypothesis that can be answered or solved. Don't go looking for shit that's not there, or shit you don't want to find."

My words are meant to be honest, but Mickey takes it as a challenge, straightening her even more and jutting out her chin.

I suck in my bottom lip to prevent myself from doing something stupid. What the fuck is with this girl that makes me want to kiss her? I felt it that night, and I'm feeling it now. And I'm not just talking about the low vibration I fell humming on my lips, compelling me to press them against hers. I'm also talking about the pulsing of my cock straining to break free of my jeans at the mere thought of kissing her. I reach up and hold her face in my hand, rubbing my thumb over her jaw. Her lips part. Her pupils dilate. I know she feels this too. We're so close I can practically taste her. I slide my hand around to her neck.

Mickey bends at the knees and ducks under my arm, turning around to face me in the center aisle. She clears her throat. "I understand why you have the pawn shop now."

I huff in annoyance, more at myself than at her. I should be grateful she pulled away when she did, but I'm not. *Trying to fuck her is not trust gaining.*

Call the Baker twins tonight. You need to fuck this chick from your thoughts. I remind myself. "You know why I have the pawn shop?" I ask. "Because I bought it from an old lady. It was an antique store. I sling dope out the back door. But you already knew that before you came storming in here to steal my shit." I grimace. "I mean, before you came in here the first time. That's not understanding me, Mic. That's doing your homework."

"I don't mean to sell…to run your side business. That wasn't what I was trying to say," she corrects herself, dropping her arms. Her blush turns crimson on her cheeks. She's embarrassed.

"I get a sick joy out of watching your face redden," I tell her, without thinking first.

Mickey looks from one wall to the other than motions to them with her hands. "All of this tells me something more. It's your unspoken story. The one I didn't know."

"This ought to be good. I'll bite. Enlighten me, Mic. Who the fuck am I now? You know, besides a kid with a learning disorder and a single guy with an ugly kitchen."

She walks down an aisle running her fingertips over various lamps and crystal bowls. She picks up a silver music box and opens it. A ballerina pops out, and the music box plays a simple lullaby.

"You lived your entire life without having much of anything."

I roll my eyes. "Telling a drug dealer they grew up without shit is like telling a stripper they have daddy issues. Come on, Mic. Impress me with that big brain of yours," I egg her on. Challenging her.

"All of these things here are pieces of lives other people have lived." She waves her hand over to the jewelry case and then the back wall. "Wedding rings. Instruments. Weapons. Rocking chairs. Paintings and portraits of families." She holds up the music box. "This probably played in a child's room at some point. Maybe, a gift from her parents or grandparents? Maybe, a reminder of a song a loved one sang to her at night." She glances from the box to me . "You had nothing growing up. No one." She slams the lid shut. "And now you have everything. Not just stuff, but pieces of a life you never got a chance to live."

Well, fuck me.

I point to her. "Let's get one thing straight. You don't fucking know me, and you never will." I run my hand through my hair. "What the fuck is it about you that makes me want to fuck you and fight you but won't fucking let me not be a fucking asshole to you."

"I don't know," she replies, softly. She places the ballerina back on the shelf. "I'm not pretending I know you, Pike. I'm just pointing out what you're silently telling the rest of the world, people who either aren't smart enough to notice, or more likely, just haven't taken the time to look." Mickey raises up on her tip-toes. "Tell me I'm wrong."

I don't know what's angering me more. The smell of the cucumber girly shampoo wafting from her hair or the heat rising from her perfect little tits as her nipples graze my chest. My cock jumps to attention, and if the wall wasn't littered with expensive instruments, I'd fucking punch a hole through it.

I lower my lips to her ear and whisper, "Fuck you."

Mickey

"What the fuck are you looking at, lady?" A boy asks, jutting out his chin and chest as if he weren't the skinniest and frailest-looking creature I've ever laid eyes on. A kitten who barks.

I open my mouth to reply, but I don't have the chance because Pike walks in. "Jo Jo! What's up, kid?"

Jo Jo drops the posturing and extends his hand out to Pike, and they do that one-shoulder half-hug that I've only seen men do.

I'm surprised that the man who tied me up in the dark with every intention of killing me gives the boy a half-hearted tap on his hat, lowering the brim over his eyes.

Jo Jo adjusts his hat and smiles at Pike like he's having a chance encounter with a celebrity. The admiration dancing in his otherwise very sad eyes.

"What brings you in, kid?"

Jo Jo shrugs. "Betty has people over tonight and told me to make myself scarce."

Pike doesn't say anything about Betty's bad parenting but instead points to the back door. "You can always hang here until the smoke settles. There's sandwich shit in the fridge upstairs if you're hungry. You know the code."

Jo Jo pats his stomach. "I'm always hungry." He starts to jog to the backdoor leading to the stairs when he pauses, once again noticing my presence. He pauses and hitches a thumb in my direction. "Pike, who's the chick with resting bitch face?"

Pike looks up at me like he, too, is just noticing that I'm here. "Right now, she's my prisoner."

"And later?" the boy asks.

Pike stares at me and blows out a breath, brushing the hair back from his forehead. "Who the fuck knows, kid."

I clench my fists. "You don't need to talk about me like I'm a dog, napping in the corner. I'm here, and I can speak for myself."

Jo Jo ignores me and scrunches up his nose. "She hanging with us tonight?"

Pike grins and leans against the glass counter, crossing his feet at the ankles. "Let's just say she ain't going anywhere."

Jo Jo shrugs as if he's accepted my less than wanted presence and again heads to the back room when his movements knocks the hat from his head. He picks it up, and when he stands, he reveals what I never thought was hidden underneath. Thick, long, wavy blonde hair.

He sets the cap backward and continues up the stairs. I look to Pike who saw the same thing I did but doesn't look the least bit surprised. When I hear the door shut, I swing my head toward Pike. "That rude little thing is a girl?" I ask, realizing how it sounds.

"What? You think only boys can be assholes? That's sexist. This is twenty-twenty. People don't think like that anymore."

"Did you just tell a joke?" I ask, cocking my head to get a better look at the abstract of a man before me, but nothing becomes clearer except that he might have undiagnosed multiple personality disorder.

"Does that offend you as well or just girls that dress like boys?" he asks, padding over to the stool.

I growl in frustration. "No, you ignorant ass. I'm not

offended, but I am surprised that she was hiding that beautiful hair under that beat-up ball cap. Or do I call her a he? How do they identify?"

Pike frowns. "Whose identifying as what? What the fuck are you talking about?"

"So much for knowing things in twenty-twenty," I mutter, then clarify. "I'm asking if the kid prefers to be addressed as he, she, or they."

Pike nods in understanding. "She, but that changes every so often."

Now, I'm the one confused. "Shit, maybe, I'm not with the times. I didn't know it can change like that."

Pike chuckles, and I grow annoyed at the enjoyment he's taking in my confusion. And even more annoyed that I wanted him to kiss me again earlier by the cello. I didn't get much sleep and couldn't even toss and turn because every time I did a part of me would come into contact with a warm muscles part of him and start the whole restless sleep all over again.

"No, Jo Jo is Josephine. She's a girl. She identifies as a girl. She likes boys, but also likes to beat them up. But she dresses as a boy or girl depending what foster home she's in and which gender will keep the creeps at bay and cause her less problems. One of the older boys likes to pick on the little boys? Then, she's a girl. If the foster dad looks at the other little girls a little too long to be parental? She's a boy. She feels out the situation within a few minutes. She's pretty talented like that, and it's kept her out of a heap of fucking trouble."

"Smart," I acknowledge. Although, I feel sad that she even has to do something as drastic as hide her gender to keep her safe.

"It is," he agrees. "She's a survivor. Just like I was. And if she ever gets into trouble she can't manage, she comes here." He takes out his phone, and that vein in his neck begins to throb. "Which reminds me." He presses a few buttons. "Hey

Badger. Pay Betty a call tonight." Pause. "No, don't tell her you're coming. Make it a surprise. She's having people over, and I know how much you love to crash a party." Pause. "No, just a small reminder of her responsibilities will work." He hangs up.

"A small reminder of what?" I ask.

"That I'm not to be fucked with." His mood is darker now. He leans over me and tilts my chin up to meet his gaze. His touch heats my skin. "Something I keep trying to teach you."

"I guess I'm not as quick of a learner as I thought," I reply.

"No," he shakes his head slowly, rubbing his thumb over my lip. "There's something that sounds a lot like pride in his voice, mixed with confusion and…lust. "No, you are not."

He removes his hand and follows Jo Jo. "Come on, Mic" he calls out, disappearing up the stairs. "Maybe, Jo Jo and I can teach you a thing or two about Monopoly."

I slide off the stool and follow. I love Monopoly and am damn good at it. I've been my family's reigning champion since I was six. There's nothing he can teach me about the board game that I don't already know.

But there is one thing I've learned today: the device on my ankle isn't a bomb. Although, that's another thing I won't be telling Pike.

CHAPTER TWENTY
PIKE

I'VE LEARNED A FEW THINGS ABOUT MICKEY OVER THE PAST FEW days.

She's a perfectionist. My entire apartment has been organized and cleaned. She even managed to get the old linoleum floor to shine when I thought it wasn't possible. She's also empathetic as all get out. Where I feel nothing, she cries at every commercial and tears up at every sighting of a stray cat. Odd for a thief and soldier of an unknown army, which is why I grow more and more intrigued about the enigma that is Mickey with each passing day.

She's also competitive as fuck, taking Jo Jo and myself all the way to the bank in Monopoly and rubbing it in our faces with a victory dance that again had my eyes fixated on what her shirt was covering.

After a long day of meetings that have me tired and irritated, I find Mickey in the alley behind the shop. She's crouched near a wall, setting out paper plates of food and Tupperware bowls of milk.

My eyes land on where the material of her pink pants stretches across her perfect heart-shaped ass. *Who is torturing who here?* "And what the fuck do you think you're doing?" My words again come out harsher than I intended. It has nothing to do with the cats, but old habits die hard, and lashing out is all I can manage to do these days. Gutter said to be nice to her. To gain her trust.

I'm fucking failing at both. Eye-fucking? Now, *that* I'm acing.

"Feeding the cats," she replies without looking up.

Adds empathetic to the list of things I've learned about Mickey.

I glance around the empty alley. "What cats?" No sooner do the words leave my lips than a half dozen of the little dirty fuckers saunter over to the bowls. Each one pausing to rub themselves against Mickey's legs before hissing claim over the food at one another.

She runs her hand across the back of a cat that I think might be white under all the grey dirt and grime. "These cats," she says with a tight-lipped smile as if she's trying not to laugh.

I raise an eyebrow and lean against the wall. "So what? You're the neighborhood cat lady now?"

She picks the smallest one of the group, cradling it in her arms and scratching behind its ears. It's beige with black ears and feet. "How would you feel if you were hungry and no one fed you?"

She's probably referring to herself during her first days here but a mental image of one of my many foster homes comes to mind. "They'll get over it and learn to fend for themselves. That's what I did."

Mickey's mouth opens, and her eyes fill with sympathy I wasn't looking for. "You've been hungry before?"

Her empathy apparently doesn't just apply to cats, it also extends to me. The man holding her against her will. I'm the last person she should feel sorry for, and yet I can feel the sorrow radiating off her skin like warmth from a buzzing fluorescent light.

I shrug and light a smoke. "Not a big deal. I wasn't the first kid, and I won't be the last."

She sets down the cat gently, parting some of the larger ones to give it access to the bowls. "Is that why you take care of Jo Jo? So that she doesn't have to go through what you went through?"

After the day I had, I'm not in the mood for her analysis, mostly because I don't need to hear my past repeated back to me. For years, I pretended it didn't exist, but Mickey has the uncanny ability to bring shit up I've been shoving down like she was there with me.

"Forget I ever said shit."

She cringes. "That's not really possible. Not with me. Good memory and all."

Right. "Fine, then pretend like I didn't say anything."

She twists her lips in thought and then flashes me a smile. A smile so unexpected and undeserved that I feel it both in my cock and in my chest. "That, I can work with."

I take another drag as the cats finish their food. When they're done they descend on Mickey who's crouching on the ground accepting their grateful gifts of affection with pure joy on her face.

She is a living, breathing crazy cat lady.

She's also going to pretend like I didn't say anything, and I'm going to pretend like this entire scene isn't fucking adorable and that her ass doesn't make me want to rip down her jeans and shove my tongue in her...I shake off the thought to make my dick calm down. The last thing I need is Mickey thinking that a bunch of cats makes me hard.

Over the past few days, I've met with leaders of several organizations with ties to Logan's Beach. Gutter tagged along, and after each meeting, he'd shake his head and say. "It ain't him, kid."

To top it all off, there's a fucking hurricane coming.

After a few days, I'm surprised that no one has come for Mickey. I haven't left her alone, but I've done as I said I would do and have dangled her like bait, giving her just enough freedom to be seen, but not converse, with dozens of customers and suppliers, even some of the ones who come through the backdoor. Not one person has recognized her and nobody's storming my shop with guns-a-blazing ready to take her back.

Maybe, I'm not the only one using her as bait. Maybe, she was meant to be left behind.

Why? I don't fucking know, but conspiracies are all I've got right now and the only explanation as to why someone would leave a soldier behind.

Music and laughter floats through the alley from Hanson's, the bar next door. Which gives me an idea. "Come on," I say, grabbing Mickey's hand and dragging her away from the cats.

"Where are we going?" she asks, reluctantly setting the runt down on the pavement. It mews as we head toward the back door of the bar. I almost feel bad for the little fucker.

"The bar?" she asks, wrinkling her nose. "Rage said it's dirty."

"Rage thinks everything is dirty. The storm's coming, and we'll be holed up for a few days. I don't know about you, but I could use a drink before that happens."

She eyes me suspiciously. "You mean not enough people have seen me dangling, and you want to make sure the gators are circling your bait?"

I open the door and wave my hand. "Smart ass," I mutter as she laughs and steps inside.

The bar is full and smells like beer-battered everything and sweat, but as we make our way to a table, the raucous laughter dies down as the head of every biker and degenerate in the place whips around in Mickey's direction. She doesn't seem to notice as she perches herself on a stool and rests her elbows on the sticky high-top table, but I know she does. She's too intuitive not to notice the whispers and appreciative glances.

Another thing I learn as I stare down every fucking biker in the place is that I'm protective of my little captive, and that the next man who eye-fucks Mic is going to get a face full of my fucking fist.

Two women I recognize and possibly have had in my bed at the same time wave at me from the bar.

"Friends of yours?" Mickey asks, rolling her eyes.

I lean in close. "Maybe. Why? Jealous?"

She doesn't hesitate. "Yes."

I blink away my surprise. Mickey is jealous. If that jealousy means she wants me as much as I want her, I'm more fucked than I initially thought. I run my hand down my face. "Of all the things you could've chosen to be honest about, that's what you fucking go with," I mutter, irritated at the throbbing in my jeans. A waitress sets two beers down on the table and leaves. I tap on the glass with my nail. "I think that's the first time you've told me the fucking truth."

She writes her name in the condensation on the outside of her beer. Her face remains expressionless yet contemplative. "In my experience, it's not lies that get you killed. It's the truth."

She's right. Irritatingly so.

I'm fixated as she trails her finger around on the bottle, drawing circles around her name. I adjust my position on the stool and avert my gaze to clear my imagination of her doing the very same thing to my cock.

I clear my throat, and Mickey looks up. She doesn't seem to notice my discomfort. She's looking elsewhere. I follow her attentions to the front window where, outside, a couple who are obviously tourists with their hats and cameras are walking on the sidewalk, hand in hand with three little girls of varying heights.

I watch her expression turn from longing to something much deeper and sadder as her eyes glass over.

"This. This wasn't a good idea." She says suddenly, pushing back her stool. It drops to the floor. She jumps over it and races out the back door.

"Mic," I yell, but she doesn't stop. I follow her only to be cut off by Gregory, one of the biggest and most annoying bikers I know. "You got a way with the ladies, eh, Pike?" He slaps my shoulder, and my entire body tenses. I flex my fingers, itching to break his fucking nose. "She's a pretty one. You tell her that I'll do right by her if she's done with you, and I promise she won't be running from—"

I see nothing but red as my fist connects with Gregory's face, knocking him into a table. The legs break, and the people sitting around it scatter as he falls along with the tabletop to the floor.

Stepping around the mess, I head for the back door.

"Usual cost for the table, Pike," Sally calls out from behind the bar.

"I'll send Thorne over," I reply. In the alley the door to the pawn shop slams and this time when I'm stopped it's not by Gregory, but by a sea of dirty mewing cats I have to step through like a furry obstacle course. "She's been here for a hot minute, and you guys take her fucking side," I mutter.

A fat black one hisses at me from the top of an overturned crate.

"Fuck you, too, asshole," I respond, giving it a middle finger.

It turns and lifts its tail, making a big production of showing me it's actual asshole. Traitors. This is my fucking alley. Not hers.

"Pike!" Thorne shouts, stepping out into the alley.

"Call an exterminator," I tell her, pointing to the cats who are now all seated and watching us quietly like we're preforming some sort of play for an army of eerie fucking cats all being puppeteered by the same master. "Why does anyone like these motherfuckers?"

"An exterminator?" She scrunches her nose. "For cats?"

"Or the humane society or that sketchy restaurant by the gas station. Anyone whose interested in getting rid of the fuckers."

"Harsh," she replies, closing the door as I push past her and head for the stairs. "I need to talk to you. And not about your odd if not emasculating issue with innocent alley cats."

"Not now, Thorne." I push past her and head for the stairs to find Mickey. "Got shit to take care of. Sally's got a bill for you. Take care of it. Four chairs and a table."

"Another one?" she huffs. "I'll take care of it, but you have to listen to me right now."

I ignore her, almost to the top of the stairs.

"Mickey's fine. She's up in the apartment. I'll check on her in a minute, but I have to talk to you. Whatever caveman reason you have to follow her up there can wait. This is more important." There's an unease in her voice, a nervousness I'm not used to hearing, at least not from her." She stomps her foot on the ground. "Pike! Stop and fucking listen to me, you big stubborn son of a bitch!"

I pause on the landing. Thorne doesn't raise her voice to me. Ever. Irritation along with concern over her sudden outburst has me turning around. I growl and thud my way down, the sound of my heavy steps echoing in the narrow stairwell.

She doesn't wait for me to reach the bottom before launching into the reason behind her outburst, besides me being an asshole as usual. "It's the hurricane," she starts. She chews on the side of her thumbnail, the other forearm wrapped around her waist, clutching at the fabric of her shirt. "It's coming to Logan's Beach. They're talking about a direct hit on the news."

I shrug. "We've been through hurricanes before. We'll handle it."

She shakes her head. "Not like this one. It's bigger and faster than they thought. It'll be here…"

The lights flicker like an ominous kick to the balls. "Soon," she finishes, as the lights buzz back to life.

It figures that the shit storm of my life now includes an actual fucking storm.

CHAPTER TWENTY-ONE
PIKE

AFTER I FINISH PREPARATIONS FOR THE HURRICANE—INSTALLING the shutters and making sure we have enough water, flashlights, and batteries to get us through the storm—I finally go in search of Mickey. Needing to know why she ran off in the bar.

And wanting to explore the jealousy thing.

The door to my apartment is open. Thorne is standing in the doorway, with arms crossed in amusement, watching as Mickey dances around the living room singing to a pop song on the radio, hiccupping between each line.

"This your doing?" I ask, pointing to the bottle of vodka in Mickey's hand.

Thorne raises her hands in self-defense and shakes her head. "Noooo. She was like this when I found her. Although, she is pretty amusing. I should have gotten her drunk earlier. She's much more tolerable when she's shit-faced."

I glare at Thorne who rolls her eyes and leaves with a middle finger salute over her head.

I close the door and lean back on it, watching the scene before me. Mickey is dancing with her eyes closed, bumping into furniture that sends her dancing back to the other side of the room. When she bumps against the wall, she starts all over again like a game of human ping-pong.

Drunken human ping-pong.

Her eyes snap open, and her smile falls as well as the lyrics on her lips. "You get those tattoos in the prison?" she asks, pointing at my neck with the hand still holding the bottle.

"Some of them. The others in juvie. Some of them King did."

"I hate them."

Nice to know.

She shakes her head, her hair swaying into her eyes. She pushes it away, and when that doesn't work, she blows at it. "I hate them because you still look beautifuls, and I nevers thought anyones was so beautifuls before, but I thinks you is. I mean. Good looking, for your sort. If you like that kind of thing and stuff. I most certainly dooooos not. Nopers. You are not sexy. I do not want to make sex with you. Not at all. Yes I do."

She's staggering, and I can't help but smile at the little drunken thief.

"You think I'm sexy?" I ask, wrapping my hand around hers, the one clutching the neck of the bottle.

She wrinkles her nose. "I thinks I just told you that I most certainly do not. Yes."

I move my hand up her arm and she doesn't try to hide her reaction. Thanks to the booze. Her lips part and her skin breaks out in thousands of little bumps. I whisper in her ear. "You want me to fuck you, Mic?"

Her face reddens, matching her already red nose. Her eyes spring open. She places a palm against my chest. Then begins to move it around cautiously at first and then a full exploration of the ridges of muscles that run down my stomach. She stills her hand then snatches it back. "I thought I was broken," she says. "I mean. I *am* broken. Never before. Never anyone but you. But now, I know I'm broken because I think you are sexaaaay when I've never found anyone sexaaaay before. I mean," she laughs and stumbles. I reach out to catch her. "Why you? Why you and all of your angry hard muscles and chiseled angry jaw line and beautiful angry eyes and kissable angry lips? Why do I want you?"

I stare at her for a few seconds because I can't find the words to reply to her admission because I have the same fucking question. "I can ask you the same thing," I finally manage to say. It helps that she's drunk and probably won't remember, so I take the opportunity to be honest and add, "Because I want you more than I've ever wanted someone in my entire fucking life."

She stares at me like she's waiting for me to say more, but there's nothing else to say. I'm confused and very aroused by the way her shirt rides up, exposing her flat toned stomach and the bottom roundness of her braless tits. I'm not going to take advantage of a drunk girl. I'm a fucking degenerate for sure, but I'm not a fucking monster.

"I don't know why you," she says and I'm not sure if it's even a question. Her eyes are wild with drunken thought and I'm pretty sure she doesn't even know if it's a question.

She shrugs casually and takes another swig, as if ignoring whatever pressing thought was running through her mind. "And I know a lot, you knows. I know everything. I don't know that. Don't know why I want you"

"I think I should get you to bed."

Her blush deepens. She wags her index finger at me. "Nah uh. No no. Just because you're handsome, and I like the way your abs do the muscle thing they do. It doesn't mean I'll go to bed with you. And you can't force me because hashtag me too and twenty-twenty and all that."

She staggers back over to me and I grab her finger, and she gasps. I understand her reaction at the simple touch because I feel it, too. Like a bolt of current shooting straight through my chest and much further south. My cock pulses beneath my jeans, and my entire body warms in a way I've never felt and do not understand.

Maybe, I'm secondhand drunk.

I take the bottle from her hands and take a swig. She whines like I've stolen her puppy. "That's miiiiyyyne."

I hold her gaze. "If it's in my apartment, it's mine."

Her eyes widen in both fear and desire, and I find myself tracing the outline of her jaw with my thumb. "Finders keepers does not apply here," she mutters. She closes her eyes and leans into my touch. "That's nice. It makes me feel tingly." Her eyes open. "All over."

"I think you need to lay down," I say, clearing my throat.

She nods and stumbles over to the couch where she falls face down onto the cushions.

I laugh. "That was graceful. Did you learn that move while you were getting your doctorate?"

The only answer I get is a soft snore, because Mickey has passed the fuck out.

CHAPTER TWENTY-TWO
MICKEY

I'M HAVING THE DREAM AGAIN.

The one where I'm drowning in murky dark water.

Only this time, it feels more real. I can taste the salty water, feel the gritty texture of the thick mud on my tongue. It runs down my throat as I will my burning lungs not to breathe it in. My eyes still as I open them, but it's no use, I can't see anything but blackness before me. As if I'm floating in the vast emptiness of space.

I'm scared. More scared than I've ever been before. My pulse races and terror sweeps through my body like an invasion of hornets stinging me into action. I'm swimming, forcing my arms and legs to move even though I'm not sure which way is up because I have to do something, and that something right now is to fight for my life, even though it seems like the outcome has already been written and the fates are laughing at me for even bothering my survival attempt.

When my hand touches the soft mud and seagrass of the river floor, I realize that hope is lost. I can't make it back the other direction. My burning lungs force my mouth open, and I inhale the thick salty water. I'm panicking when I'm suddenly ripped from the river. Not by someone coming to my rescue, but by a sound. A loud bang.

I wake up with a start, clutching my throat and gasping for air as if I've finally broken through the surface. It's still dark, and I can't see anything in front of my face, but reality calms me as I realize that I'm not in the water at all. It was just a dream. I'm in bed.

After a few seconds, I'm able to calm my breathing. I run my hands over the mattress around me, and the ebbing fear roars back to life.

I'm in a bed, but it isn't mine.

A large masculine body stirs beside me, rinsing away the grogginess of sleep and reminding me of where I am and who I'm with.

Pike.

A large bang against the window makes me jump. My head pounds with a reminder of how much I drank last night. Or this morning. I don't know what time it is because there's no light shining through the windows, now covered with what looks like corrugated metal hurricane shutters.

The shutters rattle on the window as the sound of the apocalypse rages outside. I begin to shiver. I've never been scared of storms before. Logically, there's no reason to be scared of wind and rain if you're inside, but this is a massive hurricane, and although Thorne explained that we're safe and prepared, I can't help but feel the opposite.

I raise my knees to my chest and try to calm my breathing.

"It's about time you woke up," a voice says. "The hurricane is almost over. You slept through most of it. We'll be fine. I had the trusses reinforced when I moved in. The structure is sound, and we aren't in a flood zone."

His words are supposed to be reassuring, but storm or not, I'm not safe.

Especially from Pike. My fear only grows as he turns to face me, the blanket dropping from his muscular bare chest. His ab muscles flex with his every movement. I shiver again, but this time for an entirely different reason.

Pike raises the blanket over my body, mistaking my shivering for chills, but I can't tolerate the confusion anymore. His comfort. I'd rather just have him punch me or stab me because him being kind to me somehow hurts worse than anything he can do to me physically.

There's pity in Pike's sleepy eyes, and I can't take it. I kick off the blankets. "I may be smart and have a good memory and like books and numbers, and I've gone through some terrible shit, but don't you ever mistake me for a pushover or someone waiting to be rescued. You don't have to pity me or feel sorry for me. I got myself into this shit, and somehow, I'll get myself out."

Pike raises his eyebrows. "Trust me. Of all the thoughts I've had about you, I've never pitied you or felt sorry for you. Not once."

"Then, why are you looking at me like that?" I shout.

"I was wondering why you ran out when you saw that family at the bar," he says. His calm demeanor as he props himself up on his elbow only irritates me more.

I shrug. "I miss my family."

"Why did you leave them in the first place?" he asks, as if it's as simple as that. "Why did they go into hiding and you didn't?"

I laugh and answer honestly. "It's complicated, but I didn't have a choice."

He stares at me silently as if he understands when he has no fucking clue what I've been through or why. "I know how that feels," he offers, and the look in his eyes tells me he's sincere.

I rest my chin on my knees again. "I can't imagine what you think of me," I laugh, but there's no humor in it. "The crazy girl who talks to her family even though they aren't here. The one who won't tell you answers you so desperately need." I look to the ceiling and sigh. "The funny thing is that I understand. If I were you, I'd hate me, too. So, don't look at me with pity because I don't deserve your pity."

Pike sits up, resting his elbows on his knees. The blanket falls further, revealing the crease between the globes of his ass and the deep V low on his waist. I avert my eyes back to the ceiling, so he doesn't catch me staring.

"You think I pity you? I don't fucking pity you, but I understand. I've done shit that I've had to do even though it was the wrong thing. Even though people got hurt." He shakes his head like he can't believe he has to explain this to me. His gaze rakes over my body. "I've thought about you a lot, Mic. Yeah, about the bullshit you're putting me through, but about other things, too." His gaze heats and so does my body. "About how your lips felt against mine when I kissed you. About how they would feel elsewhere on my body. About how you would taste, everywhere. About how I could make you scream my fucking name and forget everything else. Even if just for a little while. But have no doubt, Mic. Of all the thoughts I've had about you, never once have I thought you were a fucking pushover."

After a lifetime of being mistaken for demure and shy because my passions lay elsewhere than in the company of others, this is the most erotic and sexually-charged thing anyone has ever said to me. So much so I tremble right down to where an ache begins to grow between my legs.

Attraction is the least logical feeling because it's not a feeling. It's a compulsion, but whatever it is, I'm compelled to want to be with Pike. To touch him and have him touch me. To explore each other further than his lips on mine. To feel him, his skin against mine.

I swallow hard as my heart begins to beat faster as my fantasy takes over my reality.

The truth is that I believe Pike, and in a way, he may not know everything, but he understands me more than anyone has before. That understanding that we share is probably what's kept me alive, as well as the cause for the awareness prickling at my body like a thousand tiny needles bringing each nerve-ending to life.

I draw up my knees to my chest, but it only awakens an aching between my legs. I feel hot. Too hot. My skin is tight. I'm struggling to keep my shit together, and every time I think I've calmed myself, my thoughts stray to Pike, and the feeling starts all over again, ten times stronger than before.

Pike's eyes darken, his lids growing hooded as if he knows exactly what I'm feeling. I need to do something because my body is on fire, and my mind is a mess. I can't think clearly, and if there's anything I hate more, it's that.

"What are you're doing to me?" Pike asks, moving closer until he's right beside me, his chest brushing my shoulder. I flush at the feel of the warmth of his hard chest against my skin and let out an audible gasp.

"I can't," I start, feeling my entire body redden. "We…we can't."

He takes hold of my knee, tugging my legs apart, gazing down between them as if I'm a feast and he's been starved his entire life. I gasp.

"I can help you," he offers. "Let me help you."

I start to protest, but he trails his fingertips along my inner thigh, and I realize I don't want to protest. I want this. I want him. It's sick and makes no sense but it's the truth.

I'm only wearing a pair of cotton panties and one of Pike's oversized white tee-shirts, and from the looks of it, he's wearing nothing at all. "You want to come so badly, don't you," he says, massaging my inner thigh. The ache is now an all-out invasion of my senses. A low roar of anticipation is building within me. Consuming me.

"Yes," I breath as his fingers graze where I want him to touch me the most.

Then, his touch is gone. My eyes meet his.

"Say it," he insists, his voice thick and rough with his own need. "Tell me Mic. Do you want me to make you come?"

Yes, yes, that's all I fucking want. Fuck everything else.

I nod.

"Tell me. Tell me that you want me to make you come," he teases, but the desire in his eyes isn't a joke. It's raw and fierce, and it sends a shock of need through my body, causing my nipples to harden against the soft fabric of my shirt. "I want to hear you say it."

"I...I want you to make me come," I manage to say, feeling both embarrassed and relieved.

Pike's smile so wicked I almost regret my admission. "Oh, Mic, what did you get yourself into?" And with those words barely out of his mouth, his lips are on mine. He rolls us so that he's on top, settled between my legs, his fingers tangled in my hair and his mouth plundering mine like he's a thief, stealing every second of the kiss as if I wasn't already giving it to him willingly.

One hand cups my ass and lifts it off the bed. His hard cock rubs against my brutally swollen clit through my panties, and I moan at the sensation and he groans, the sound making me open my eyes and look up at this man whose usually very controlled, but now, with his hair mussed and that look in his burning eyes, he seems wild, like a caged animal just set free.

He strokes me again. An assault to my senses. Over and over his hard shaft thrusts against me until I'm lifting my hips on my own accord, trying to take what I need, what I can't seem to find on my own. "Oh, no, not yet," Pike teases, pausing his movements.

"This is a different kind of torture," I groan.

"You don't know shit about torture...yet," he says, lowering himself down on my body until his face is level with the most intimate parts of me, spread open for full view. He inhales deeply, and I don't have time to be embarrassed by what he's just done because his mouth is on me, lightly at first, just a kiss as if he were kissing my lips. His tongue circles my clit, and he sucks ever so lightly on the sensitive flesh. He finds a pattern that makes me gasp and moan. Circling, sucking and releasing until I'm panting like an animal.

"You know what I hate about you the most?" he suddenly asks, staring up at me from between my legs.

I shake my head as I try to catch my breath, not able to wrap my head around what's happening, never mind what he's asking. My entire body is thrumming with need, wanting for more.

He raises up on his knees, covering my body once again with his. He traces his fingers from my collar bone between my breasts, circling my belly button.

His voice is still rough but somehow softer around the edges. "What I hate about you most…" his eyes meet mine. "Is that I don't hate you at all." Pike brushes a hair from my face. "You belong to me," he says, as if it's a fact I should already know. His gaze is heated and determined. His bare chest rising and falling with each angry breath. "You have since that first night."

The idea that I belong to anyone heats my blood. I've spent too much time pretending to be a part of people I hate. "I'm not one of your possessions from the pawn shop. You didn't buy me, and I'm not something that got left behind."

He quirks a brow. "Aren't you?"

I realize the irony in what I'd just said. *I was left behind.*

"You know it's not the same," I say, snapping my teeth at his lips as he tries to come closer for another kiss.

He pins my arms down, and his face is inches from mine. "You're not an object to me. You're not a possession, but I own you in a way I've never wanted to own something before. I don't want you on display or on my shelves for others to look at. To touch. And I sure as shit don't want to sell you to someone else."

"Then, what do you want from me?" I ask, hating the tears that threaten to fall from my eyes.

He grabs my chin, forcing me to look at him. "Fuck, Mic, I want *you*."

He's stripping me bare, and I don't just mean my just clothes. But as one layer comes and then another so do my inhibitions, and when he pulls me against his chest and we're warm skin against warm skin, I realize I've never felt more free than I do right now, fully exposed to Pike, naked in his arms.

"Fuck, you're perfect," he groans.

It's the adrenaline, I tell myself, that has the air shifting all around us. I don't have time to ask who or what is happening because the second my lips part to speak, Pike descends on me, covering my lips with his.

I don't know if we're fighting or kissing, but it's aggressive and passionate. Our tongues warring with one another. I moan into his mouth.

"What are we doing?" I ask, breathlessly.

"I don't fucking know," Pike answers, pressing his lips to mine once more. He grinds his shaft where I need it most, and I see stars. I lift my hips, seeking more of a connection. Lifting me so that I'm straddling him, his massive cock jutting between us. I grind down against him as his lips suck and kiss my neck and jaw. "Whatever it is. It feels so fucking good. You feel so fucking good, Mic."

Our eyes meet.

I have no doubt that if our lust were flammable, the slightest spark would burn us both alive.

He flips me over, pressing my chest to the mattress. He

kneads my ass with his fingers, rubbing his cock between my ass cheeks.

I groan and arch my ass toward him, but he's gone. Only cool air licks my skin. His fingers dig into my shoulder, and the air shifts around us from lust to something much more sinister. I still, knowing exactly what he's found.

Shit. Shit Shit.

"What the fuck is this?" he grates flipping me over to face him. He hovers above me with both hands on the mattress beside my head.

"It's nothing. It's…" But I know it's too late. I know I've been found out. My lust-addled brain lapsed for one second and showed him everything I'd been working so damned hard to conceal. It's over now. There's no going back from this. Whatever Pike and I just started, will never be finished.

"It's a fucking brand," he says through gritted teeth. He pushes off the bed and stands at the edge, his erection is thick and hard despite the anger in his voice and the tension in his shoulders.

I grab for the t-shirt and toss it back over my head.

"Fuck this. Fuck you. I can't…" Pike doesn't finish his thought. He shakes his head and tugs on his jeans. I want to explain. I want to tell him everything, but the words don't come. I feel the gap between us widening, the connection we shared severing as he turns and walks to the door. He pauses with his hand on the doorknob. "Ahhhhhhhhhhh!" Rearing back, he slams his fist through the wall with an angry roar tearing from his chorded throat that I can I feel as if I were the one screaming.

My spine jumps as the door slams shut, leaving me alone while the storm continues raging outside and a new kind of torturous pain weaving its way through what's left of my heart.

CHAPTER TWENTY-THREE
PIKE

"You awake, sleepy head?" Nine asks, staring down at me.

Great, for the fucking second time, I had the fucking dream. What a way to start out the fucking day. Oh, that and remembering the fucking brand I discovered on Mickey's shoulder.

I shift to a sitting position and rub my eyes, my back aches from sleeping on the cot in my office. There's a pool of sweat on the cot, and more of it that drips down my back, but it's expected since the A/C doesn't run without power.

It's been years since I've had that dream. A memory of the first time in my life I ever felt betrayed. After that moment, my entire life has been governed by one fucking rule.

Don't let your guard down.

It was either the attempt to gain Mickey's trust that did me in, or if it was more primal, my body responding to the overwhelming desire that's been building for Mickey over the past few weeks, but somewhere I'd let my guard down and I'd let her in. Enough so that when I saw the mark on her shoulder, I felt more than anger.

I was...hurt.

Which is ridiculous since there's no reason for me to feel

hurt. It was eventually going to come down to this moment whether I saw the mark or not, but still, I wasn't prepared for the boulder dropped on my chest at the sight of the Four branded into her fucking skin like a fucking farm animal.

Nine leans against my desk. "The hurricane's over. Your shingles are a little fucked, and a tree fell into one of the warehouse panels, but other than that, you made it through better than most of the fuckers in this town. I almost didn't make it through with all of the flooding. The roads are fucked, too. Trees and power lines are down everywhere. Preppy told me that King's house is a shit show, so consider yourself lucky."

When I don't answer, Nine looks me over, twisting his lips. "No offense, dude, but you look like shit. What the fuck has been going on over here? Where's Mickey?" He looks around my empty office and through the hall to equally empty pawn shop.

"Everything fucking happened here," I grumble, pushing my hair back on my head.. "Mickey is upstairs, probably sewing my sheets into hoods."

"Uh, care to elaborate? Or is she just really into crafting now?"

I blow out a long breath, light a cigarette and tell him everything.

When I finish, Nine just stands there looking like he's been electrocuted. "Mickey? Mickey's a fucking racist?" He sits on the edge of my desk and lights a joint, taking a deep drag.

"It appears so." I take a hit of the joint he hands me and pass it back. "Of all of the fucking degenerates in this town, she has to be a part of the fucking Fourth Reich. The worst of them all. Their hatred doesn't come from business dealings gone wrong or for protection, but from ignorance. The worst kind of criminal is an ignorant one."

"Here here, brother. I wholly agree."

Thorne walks in and slams down a Styrofoam tray on my desk. Coffee splashes out from the top of the four cups, splattering on my lap. I wipe it off my jeans with my hand.

Thorne makes no effort to help me clean it up or apologize. Instead, she stands with her shoulders back and places her hands on her hips. Her belly ring charm sways with the motion. It's purple and sparkly and says *fuck you*. "She's not a fucking racist, you morons."

"Why hello to you, too," I mutter, removing the least messy coffee from the tray. "How did you fare in the storm? We're okay, thanks for fucking asking."

She shrugs. "I'm alive. My apartment is on the third floor, so we're all good. But I wanted to come and check on you, and it turns out you look worse than the fucking roads do." She takes a sip of her own coffee in reusable mug that says I HATE YOU. Thorne apparently has a theme today. "So, where was I?" she puts a finger to the corner of her lips. "Oh yeah, now I remember," she slams her palms on my desk, rattling the coffee once again. "Mickey isn't a racist."

"The brand on her shoulder says otherwise," I offer, wishing the weed would work faster so I could bury my confusion in my high instead of trying to find answers to questions that don't make any fucking sense. "Besides, how would you fucking know?"

Thorne juts out her chin. "My grandfather was a Grand Dragon in the Klan."

Nine sprays his coffee all over the floor. "Excuse me? Como say the fuck WHAT?"

Thorne rolls her eyes. "So dramatic," she says, lowering herself in her chair. She pulls out her phone, and her thumbs fly over the screen. "Thankfully, the cell tower is still up. Ah, here we go." She turns the screen to me, pointing to a picture of a man wearing a Klan robe and white witch-like hat. The standard uniform of ignorance. "This was him. My Popop. Loved us and hated pretty much everyone else."

"So, your grandfather was a piece of shit, and that somehow doesn't make Mickey a piece of shit?" Nine questions.

She rolls her eyes. "I grew up with the language of hate. The words. The propaganda. The feelings they try to instill in you. Hate is something that's taught. It's not something we instinctually have toward others. There wasn't one-word Mickey spoke or action she took to make me believe she's racist. I pick up on those things and trust me, she didn't exhibit a single one of them. I was brought up and taught hate, but it never sunk in. I loved my Popop, but I never believed what he did. Not for one second. I think Mickey's the same. She may wear the mark, but that's exactly what it is. Just a mark. Something on the surface that only goes skin deep. Like a tattoo in Chinese letters that you think says love and light but really says ham sandwich."

Nine laughs. "So what you're saying is, just because she has ham sandwich tattooed on her body, doesn't mean she loves ham sandwiches." He scratches his head. "But everyone loves ham sandwiches. It's a proven fact. Science and shit. Mickey would know. I'll ask her."

"Maybe, she's a good actress?" I reply, wanting to feel anger more than hurt, looking for reasons to drag that anger from beneath the pain and use it to put my shield back in fucking place where it belongs.

Thorne shakes her head. "She's been kind to Jo Jo even when Jo Jo wasn't kind to her." She pulls the necklace out from her shirt and holds up the pendant. It's the Star of David. "When she saw this, she didn't bat an eyelash."

"Why do you wear a Star of David if your Popop was in the clan?"

"It's my girlfriend's. She gave it to me. The point is that hate is an agenda. Those fuckers are preachy. Whatever reason she has for being a part of the Fourth Reich has nothing to do with hatred of others."

Something occurs to me. "Not of the racist kind, anyway."

"What are you thinking?" Nine asks. We're interrupted when his phone rings. He picks it up, pacing the room. "Hold on, I'll put you on speaker," he says, clicking a button and setting the phone down on the counter. "Go ahead, King."

"Whoever is after me sent my daughter's crazy biological mother after my kid during the storm. Almost killed my wife and both of my daughters," King grates. "We took down several of their hired guns but none of them talked before they died except to say your fucking name, Pike. This shit ends, and it ends now. Find out who is behind this, and why they want to take you down and everyone else around you, then give me a fucking name. No one involved in this is left breathing, you understand me?"

Thorne gnashes her teeth and slips into the back room, and I wish I could go with her.

Nine and I exchange looks. He raises his eyebrows silently asking, *Are you going to tell him about her?*

"Understood," I say, my neck and shoulders tightening with tension and anger. I look to the stairs. "I've got a lead. I'll let you know what comes of it."

The line goes dead.

"I'll tell him," I say to Nine, rubbing my eyes, "when there's something concrete to tell."

Now that I know who Mickey really is, I realize the entire time she's been playing a game with me, regardless of her reasons. A part of me wishes I never saw that mark, but I did and there's no coming back from it. But there are two players in her game.

And I never lose.

She wants to play?

I'll play. And I'll fucking win.

"Call Darius Alban," I tell Nine. "Arrange a trade. The girl for a truce."

He tucks his phone in his pocket. "You really want a truce and not mass murder?"

"The trade is only the setting," I crack my knuckles. "For the mass murder."

CHAPTER TWENTY-FOUR
PIKE

NINE FOLLOWS ME UP THE STAIRS, AND I'M READY TO DO BATTLE OR worse when I smash open the door, but Mickey is in a heap on the floor, sobbing. She looks up at me with tear-filled eyes. My chest tightens at the site of her so sad, weak, vulnerable like I've never seen her before. What happened to the brave girl who was ready to take on whatever I was prepared to give?

I came up here ready for war and she's already collateral damage.

I remind myself that she's not my Mic anymore. She never really was. She's a soldier of the Fourth fucking Reich.

Nine looks to me, but I can't speak so he speaks for me. He tells Mickey everything King just said about his wife and children being in danger and about the woman the Fourth Reich sent after them.

She rises to her knees and wipes the hair from her eyes. There's no need to threaten her because I see in the way her shoulders have slumped over that she's already given up. Her eyes meet mine. "I'll tell you everything. It's time. I'm hurting people by not telling the truth. Not just you. Kids. I can't...I can't do this anymore."

Nine sits on the dresser, and sets his gun beside him, keeping it within reach.

I lift Mickey off the floor and place her on the bed, but she instantly stands, shaking free of my grip. She walks to the window and I perch at the end of the bed, ready to hear what it is she has to say.

After a few seconds, she takes a deep breath and speaks to us while still looking out the window. "My dad wasn't an affectionate man, but we never doubted that he loved us. He gave us everything he could to my sisters and my mother and me. He was never cruel. But he wasn't an open book either. He was secretive. His praise and compliments were limited to our accomplishments and never given for our character. My sisters all succeeded in different areas. I think to some point it was to please him, because they saw all of the attention he gave me when I won an award or was the youngest person to receive a doctorate of science in my university. Although they got the praise, it was never like the kind he gave me. Maybe, it was because we were in the same field. But regardless, with any of us, it was never the kind of attention or pride that ended with an *I love you*. To the point where my sisters and I clung to every little endearment he offered as if it were the hugs we so desperately craved. But we loved him despite, and possibly in spite, of it."

"Let's jump forward a bit. Why the Fourth Reich? I mean, I've got a lot of reasons to hate a lot of people, but race isn't one of them," Nine remarks, jumping ahead in the story. "Basically, my question is, when did you become a hateful bitch and why?" He points at her. "And go."

"I'm not a racist," she insists. "I have the same hate in my heart that they do, but the only group of people I hate as whole are them."

Nine raises his hand. "Uh, professor, I'm a little lost here. Can you please explain? Examples? Answer key? Anything?"

"Put your fucking hand down," I mutter.

Mickey paces around the room, wringing her hands. "I've been training as a soldier in the army of the Fourth Reich for four years. Little did they know what they've been training me for."

"What exactly is that?" Nine asks.

She spins around and I'm trapped in her gaze. "Justice. They were training me, and I was going to use that training on them and get much deserved much needed justice."

"You mean revenge," I argue.

She nods. "In this case, they are one in the same. Although justice makes it sound more superhero and less…"

"Like premeditated murder?" Nine finishes.

"I guess you can say that," she replies, on a laugh, nervously shaking out her hands. "Because it's true. No matter what words you use."

I lean forward, resting my elbows on my knees. "Revenge for what?" I ask, because I need to fucking know.

"It's a really long story," she replies, her eyes glassy with unshed tears.

"We ain't going nowhere. Tell us," I probe, needing to understand her affiliation with the racist bastards. I look to Nine. "No interrupting. Let her fucking speak."

She thinks for a few beats. "My father was in the same field of study that I'm in. *Was* in. He went undercover before I was born in the Fourth Reich. The took us, the whole family, to their gatherings. We all repeated the sick chants. Cheered at the propaganda. At night, when we were home, he'd tell us how successful his research was and that we were a big part of that success. All we had to do was keep playing our part, and we'd all be rewarded when his research landed him a guest spot on CNN and a book turned into a movie. His delusions of grandeur were so big it made him greedy. It made him stay long after he should have pulled out."

I resist placing my hand on her thigh because as much as I want to comfort her, she doesn't deserve my comfort, and I can't risk what touching her again might do to my resolve to see this thing through. "What happened? What went wrong?" I ask.

She looks to the ceiling as if the answer is taped to it. "I don't know the details, but they must have found out who my father really was and what he was doing there. Twenty years is a long time, and I don't think they liked the idea that they were taken for fools for that long. I remember when my father came back to the beach house one day looking frazzled. Scared. We had to leave really fast. We didn't even pack. We just got in the van and took off." She takes her eyes from the ceiling and looks to me.

"They caught up to us. There was gunfire. My sisters screamed. My mother's face was the palest I'd ever seen. She was terrified. There was a noise like a crushing pop, and then my mother's face was splattered with red.

"My father...he'd been shot in the head. He was dead. My mother tried to take hold of the wheel, but his foot was pressed up against the gas. There was nothing she could do.

We blew through the guardrail. There was so much screaming. The water was too fast. Too deep. I screamed for my mother, but she didn't answer. My sisters...they were all contorted, and I don't know if they were still alive, but they weren't conscious. There were no more screams. I tried to feel for a pulse on my sister Mindy, but the water was up to my neck and then over her head, and I couldn't feel anything."

She smiles at me through her tears, and I want to fucking kill every single person whose ever caused her to cry. "You found me that night and took me home. I was delirious. It didn't hit me—what happened—until they started shooting at us on the beach. I surrendered because I didn't want you to die for the sins of my father."

"What happened after they took you?" I ask, realizing now it wasn't a rescue after all.

"Psychology happened. When Darius saw me, I knew he was ready to kill me. But the only reason he'd have for wanting me dead would be if I believed he was the villain, the man who killed my family." She takes a deep breath to steady herself. "So, when I saw him for the first time, I wrapped my arms around him and cried to Uncle Darius that we were in a car accident because someone ran us off the road and shot at us and that I was so glad to see that he was okay because I feared whoever killed my family might've been after him, too. And I thanked him for rescuing me."

"And he believed you?" Nine asks.

"I didn't give him a reason not to believe me. I let him believe he was the savior in my story, and he, in turn, filled the role."

I clench my fists, understanding and sympathy flooding past any fucking guard I've been trying to build between us. "Jesus Fucking Christ. You put yourself in a pen with the fucking wolves."

She sits on the bed, and I can't help myself. This time, I place my hand on her thigh and give it a squeeze. She doesn't flinch although her eyes widen with surprise. *You and me both*, I silently tell her, feeling her muscle relax under my touch.

"No, I didn't put myself in the pen with them," she explains. "I became a wolf. At least, as far as they were concerned."

"So, your plan was to kill them?" I ask.

She nods. "Each and every one of them, starting at the bottom and working my way up. It's not a quick death. It's more like a biological weapon. I wanted to kill them from the inside, slowly and painfully. The entire organization as a whole. I didn't want to take their lives I wanted to take their trust in the Fourth Reich, their beliefs, everything that held them together, but first, I had to gain their trust. Follow their orders. Darius even went as far as to feed me a lie of who was really responsible for my parents' death."

"Who?" I ask, squeezing her thigh again.

She glances up at me. "You."

I stand like I've been shot at. "That motherfucker!"

"It's not like I believed him," she assures me. "I knew it was Darius all along, and I know he has an agenda that has to do with destroying you that has nothing to do with how he destroyed my family. He was just feeding me a lie to fulfill that agenda so I let him think I believed him."

"Percy," I mutter. "The fucker thinks it's me that got him locked up all those years ago."

"That actually makes fucking sense," Nine replies. "It's not like we've ever done business with them. They'd have no other reason to hate us. I mean, I don't know if you've noticed but we're white as fuck. Embarrassingly so."

"I thought as much," Mickey says with a sniffle. "But I know it wasn't you who ratted on him."

"How?" I ask, pausing my furious pace of the room.

"Because…it was me."

Mickey

"Because it was me," I say with both pride and regret filling my voice. "My father and Darius always pushed us, Percy and me, together in hopes that we'd be the new faces of the Reich. Of course, my father told me it was all part of his research, and I agreed to whatever he proposed, in the name of knowledge. His research was important. He was always so close to the end. To finding out what made the human brain hate."

"He let you get close to a fucking monster," Pike growls, his neck chording with anger. A vein in his forearm pulses under a tattoo of the name *Greyson*.

I nod. "He had me visit him in the detention center once, and while I was there, I was approached by the FBI. I was young and scared, and they threatened to put away my father, but the real reason I wore that wire is because it felt like the right thing to do. Now, looking back…" I can no longer help the tears that stream down my face. "It's probably what led to Papa being found out, and my entire family being killed."

Pike drops to his knees before me. "It wasn't your fucking fault," he says, grabbing my hands in his. "None of this was your fucking fault," he says the words with so much passion and determination that I almost believe him, but being the logical person I am, facts are facts. My actions may have led to my father's death.

Nine is typing furiously on his laptop. He finally looks up, and his expression is one of confusion. "You said your father was undercover? That's what he told you?" Nine asks.

"Yeah, why?" I ask, hesitantly.

Pike rises to his feet but keeps my hand clasped in his.

Nine brings his laptop over and sets it down on the bed. "Because this says otherwise." It's an article. A newsletter rather. I recognize it as propaganda of the Fourth Reich. There's a picture of a much younger Darius with another man whose eyes are the same grey shade as mine.

I gasp and feel my face pale. No, this can't be true. It can't be. I jerk my hand from Pike's and walk over to the window.

"What?" Pike growls at Nine.

I can feel Pike's eyes on me as Nine answers. "This is from over thirty years ago, not twenty. Mickey's father wasn't under-cover in the Fourth Reich." Nine taps on the screen. "He was a founding member."

CHAPTER TWENTY-FIVE
MICKEY

I FIND THORNE IN THE OFFICE.

Pike and Nine are upstairs huddled together to make sense of this mess I made, and I couldn't stand it any longer. I was choking on my own sadness and guilt.

I know they told Thorne everything because I'd heard them downstairs. The look Thorne gives me when I enter isn't one of hatred or pity but sympathy.

"I'm curious," she says. "How does that photographic memory thing of yours work?"

I'm grateful for the question, any question about anything other than about my current situation. I answer immediately. "Think of it this way: if you read a page in a book, you see black letters on a white page. I may know it's black letters on a white page, but I interpret them as white letters surrounding them in black. It's how my brain is able to process more than one thing at once."

She shrugs. "Guess you never had to study much."

I twist my lips and think. "Yes, and no. I can take a quick glance at the text book and memorize the answers, but to truly learn something and know it without having to revert to that particular memory, I have to read it a few times, just like everyone else, and in that way, yeah, I still have to study. There's a big difference between knowing something and truly understanding the meaning behind it."

"Is there a downside?" she asks.

Only remembering everything you never wanted to remember in vivid fucking detail. "Several. Sometimes, I have a hard time following conversation. Things get cluttered in my brain. Let's say my parents started talking about going back to a restaurant we went to last summer on our vacation. Well, my brain automatically opens the album under the file for that restaurant, and I lose the rest of what they're saying because I'm too busy remembering how the waiter had a patch of hair under his ear by his jawline he missed while shaving, or how the awning has a tear on the left side under the letter A in the restaurant's name, or how the bathroom stall had an advertisement on the door for an entirely different establishment selling the same kind of food, and then I'm reciting the phone number of the competition out loud, and when I'm done, I come to and my parents and sisters are all staring at me, waiting for me to come back to earth and out of my own junkyard of a brain."

"How do you deal with it?" she asks, seemingly genuinely interested.

"How does anyone deal with anything?" I reply, looking to the fluorescent lights on the ceiling as the buzz to life.

"Generator must have kicked in," Thorne says. "Keep going."

"I don't, really. I just live. I believe that it's a gift for the most part and it makes me, well… me."

For a moment, I wander around the office while Thorne works. This could be the last time I see her, and something about her has been marinating in my brain.

"When are you going to tell Pike?" I ask, shoving my hands into my back pockets.

"Tell him what?" She snaps her eyes to mine.

"That you're his sister."

Her jaw drops. "How...how did you know?" She rubs the birthmark behind her ear.

I smile. "You mean from besides the fact that you both make the same expression when you're worried about something but trying not to look like you're worried?" I ask. "Or the moon shaped birthmark you both have behind your left ears?"

She realizes what she's doing and stops.

"Why haven't you told him?" I press.

Thorne sighs, mindlessly swiveling in her chair. "You know how he is. He isn't into family. When I found out about him, I came to tell him, and when I started talking about family to lead up to telling him, he told me that family meant nothing to him. That it's a bullshit pretend bond people lean on to make excuses for their lives. He really didn't leave much of an opening, and it kind of never came up again."

"And you want to mean something to him," I realize out loud.

She smiles. "I did. And I do."

"Weren't you worried that he'd be attracted to you? Try something with you?" I ask, curious. She's a beautiful girl, and Pike...well, he's Pike. My stomach twists with regret and pain at what I've done and what I've yet to do.

Her eyes widen. "Um. Ew. No," she says, but then sighs when I don't accept her simple answer. "There is no attraction between us, and I know he feels it, too, but just in case, I had a contingency plan."

"Which was?"

She smiles brightly. "I told him I was a lesbian. And while I do have a roommate, she's my best friend, but she plays the part well when he's around."

I laugh. "Ah, good call."

She looks me over. "You know, we aren't that different. We

both want to be a part of his life, but telling him how much he really means to us could destroy everything."

"But I—"

My protest is cut off by the bells above the door ring.

"Saved by the bells," Thorne says, pushing past me into the pawn shop. "See ya later. Gotta take care of this electric bullshit. See if it's ever going to come back on." She looks back at me. "For what it's worth, I never thought you were a racist, which is why I didn't tell Pike about the mark the first night I saw it."

She walks into the other room, leaving me in a state of shock.

She knew. This entire time, Thorne knew.

I head back up the stairs, sparing one more glance for Thorne who's conversing with an electrician in a hard hat, carrying a clipboard. She's the first person in years I would consider a friend. I'm going to miss her more than I want to admit to myself.

Goodbye, Thorne

On my way back up the stairs, I'm surprised to hear noise from a room I assumed was storage. The door is cracked, so I listen. "The trade goes down two days from today at the warehouse in Coral Pines," I hear Pike say.

"The girl for a truce?" I recognize the voice as King.

"That's what Darius agreed to," Pike answers, as my heart breaks wide open in my chest. It's only partially because he's so willing to trade me because my logical side should have seen that coming, but it's because he thinks that Darius Alban would actually agree to a truce when I know in my heart it will be an ambush.

"I'll call the boys. We'll all be waiting there for them. They'll get what's coming to them, and The Fourth Reich will be a distant memory in Logan's Beach come Saturday fucking morning," King says.

Apparently, they're planning an ambush of their own.

I can't let this happen. I can't let more people die. I have to get back to the Fourth Reich and press fast forward on my plans.

I pad over to the apartment and enter Pike's room without so much as making the door creek. I rush over to the safe that's acting as a nightstand, and I get to work on cracking it.

CHAPTER TWENTY-SIX
MICKEY

"I know you heard us, and it's not what you think!" Pike angrily calls from the other side of the locked door.

It's exactly what I think. They're about to go get themselves killed although he thinks I've barricaded myself in his room because I heard him talking about trading me when really, I'm just buying myself some time.

Finally, on the three-thousandth try, the safe opens, and what I need is right there on the first shelf beside a stack of cash. I leave the cash, but take the gun. I check to make sure it's loaded.

It is.

I push myself into the furthest corner of the room.

"I know you have my fucking gun. You may be smart, but I'm not fucking stupid. Cameras, remember? If you think you're leaving with it or at all, you're fucking wrong." He pounds against it again. "Open the goddamn door, Mic!" he yells. The anger and hurt in his voice pierce my chest, and I feel it as if it's my own.

For a few seconds, I think he's left because I hear nothing but the sound of my own rapid breathing. Until the door smashes in, pushing the dresser I'd placed in front of it just enough to create a small path.

Pike's massive body stands in the shadowy doorway, his anger radiating off of him like toxic chemicals rising into the air.

I hold my breath and steel my nerves. Pike steps in, bare-chested and glistening with sweat. His jeans are undone and low on his waist, exposing the band of his black boxer briefs.

I raise the gun in both hands, aiming it at his chest. "I have to go. You can't stop me," I say, with all the resolve I have left. "You're going to trade me and ambush them, but don't you think they have the same plans for you? I have to go, and that way, less people will die. YOU won't die. So, just let me leave. I have a plan. It will work. I'll take them down for both of us."

"No." Pike looks from me to the gun. "And as I've told you before, you're not going anywhere." His words are dark and menacing. An amused smile turns up the corners of his lips.

It's infuriating. He's infuriating.

I straighten my shoulders. "What's so funny?" I ask, swallowing down the rising fear in my throat. I remind myself of one important fact to keep from choking on that fear.

I'm the one holding the gun.

Instead of freezing or retreating as one would do in this situation, Pike takes a bold step forward, catching me off guard. I stagger backward, but I'm not fast enough. He reaches out, and at first, I think he's going for the weapon, but he doesn't. He confuses me as he wraps his hands around mine, tightening my grip around the gun. He lifts my hands and bends slightly at the waist, forcefully pressing the barrel against his forehead. "You wanna shoot me, Mic? Then, fucking shoot me," he dares, with wild blood shoot eyes.

My mouth drops open, but words don't come out. I expected Pike to defend himself. To come at me. To step aside and let me leave, even though it was the least possible of all the outcomes. I didn't plan for this.

I can do this. I have to do this.

"Not what you were expecting?" His tone is both mocking and rage-filled. "I know what that pretty brain of yours is thinking. You want me to attack you and make pulling the trigger easier on that conscious of yours." He bites out a laugh. "Not gonna happen. If you want to do this, I'm not going to stand in your way, but you're not fucking leaving either. So, come on. Shoot me. Go ahead. Do what you planned to do." His eyes narrow with determination. My hands shake in his. "Pull the fucking trigger!"

The air around us is thick and charged. My skin breaks out in a sheen of sweat. My adrenaline spikes, and I feel all too alert. Too aware of what's taking place between us.

I grip the gun tighter and gaze into his dark eyes, his pupils are large and covering every hint of color within them. Behind the anger and determination, there's something else that I didn't expect. Something that I'm all too familiar with. Hurt. Pain that mirrors my own. Desperation that calls out to me like a piece of my soul trapped within Pike.

"Shoot me!" he cries, his face red with anger, teeth bared like a wild animal. "Fucking shoot me!"

With those words, my fiery resolve dissolves into ash.

I step back, needing to put some distance between us, but Pike doesn't have the same thought. He follows me backward, keeping his grip tight on my hands and the gun between them.

"I…I can't do this," I whisper, releasing my grip on the gun.

Pike releases his hold on me, catching the gun before it can fall to the floor.

Shit.

I look to the window, but it's too high, and Pike is directly in front of the only door. There's no escape. So much for being brave. Instead, I've signed my own death warrant. My heart races erratically with the realization that this is it. It's over.

I'm over.

"This was a really stupid fucking move for someone who claims to be so smart, " Pike sneers. He raises the gun.

I pinch my eyes shut, waiting for the bullet of his wrath to pierce my skin. I hear a thud, and my eyes fly open and land on the carpet where Pike's tossed the gun to the floor.

My eyes meet his in silent question. Why?

He answers by charging, a one-man stampede I can't avoid as he barrels toward me. His chest crashes against mine, and my head connects with the wall with a thud that rattles my bones. I'm dizzy as fear lands in my gut like a ball of fire. My pulse races as his closeness consumes me. The smell of cologne and cigarettes lingers between us—a trace of whiskey on his breath.

"You're going to regret not pulling that trigger," he sneers. The darkness in Pike's eyes tells me that, gun or no gun, I'm not getting out of this unpunished.

Or possibly even alive.

I swallow hard.

He cages me in with his hands against the wall beside me, engulfing me in the heat and rage radiating from his hard body. I feel his heart beating fast beneath his chest now pressed against mine. "What to do with you now?" Pike muses, his breath ragged. His voice full of promise and warning. He brushes his lips over my temple. I tremble at the contact. "You're going to pay for that little stunt, Mic."

He's close. Too close. I'm entirely rigid, frozen in place. This wasn't supposed to happen. How did I let this happen? I'm the most terrified I've ever been, and yet there's something else I can't understand. Something else between us that's charging the air, causing me to shake, and it's not just from fear. Hatred mixed with need. The yearning I've denied for him is no longer lying dormant. It's as real as the ache growing in my stomach, the wetness between my thighs. If I thought the room felt charged before, it's damn near on fire now. The flames of desire and hate lick at the walls around us, setting everything ablaze, making the small room feel smaller, closing in around us.

My nipples harden as they brush against his chest. I suck in a gasp.

He doesn't miss my reaction. He looks to where my nipples are straining against my shirt with heated eyes.

The only sound in the room is our mutual heavy breathing as he slowly pulls his gaze from my chest. His eyes lock on mine. For a few seconds, we just stare at each other—foreheads lined with confusion and anger.

A silent dare.

My mind, on the other hand, is anything but silent.

"Should I kill you or fuck you?" he muses. And I'm honestly not sure what scares me more. His anger or his desire. He brushes the backs of his knuckles against my jaw. "Maybe, both."

"What do you—" I don't have time to finish my question because his lips are on mine. He hoists me in the air, and my legs wrap around his waist on instinct.

It's an angry joining of clacking teeth and biting lips. A war we are still fighting both with each other and ourselves. He growls at me when I pierce his lip, drawing blood. He licks the blood with his tongue then kisses me again, this time harder. A punishing kiss that has me growling at him in return. His coppery blood on my tongue tastes like victory. He licks his way between my lips, pushing his tongue into my mouth, licking and devouring with rough determined strokes. With a jerk of his hips, he presses the massive erection beneath his jeans between my legs, the pleasure that courses through me has me momentarily seeing stars. I grind down on him in return.

He hisses in response, baring his teeth against my lips. "You're going to pay for that, Mic," he warns, taking my mouth in another kiss that has us grunting and growling at one another like starved animals fighting over the last scrap of food. But neither of us is about to give up. He pushes me back onto the bed, falling with me over my body, my legs splayed on both sides of his hips as he presses his cock again between my legs. I arch my back, needing to feel more. Needing for there to be nothing between us but desire. For each other, and to win. But, this is no longer a game we're playing. It's a battle. A war neither of us can win.

But, one in which we will both go down fighting.

He sits up on his knees, exposing the deep cut lines of muscle beaded with sweat. I dart out my tongue to taste his salty skin. He closes his eyes with a groan, then reaches behind me, pulling me up into a sitting position long enough to rip the shirt over my head and toss it to the floor with his own. He presses between my breasts, sending me back down to the mattress then yanks my shorts and panties off with one pull. I feel the air on my naked skin for a brief moment and a flash of terror bolts through my chest.

Pike covers me again with his body, his bare chest against mine is a sensation like I've never felt. Hard against soft. My nipples ache beneath his warm skin. His cock is hard and hot beneath his jeans as he pushes against my clit causing a ripple of pleasure to course through me. I shudder as my pussy clenches at emptiness, and I groan as the ache demands to be sated as my body demands to be filled.

I rake my nails over Pike's back, punishing him for not being inside me. Punishing him for making me want him, for making me afraid to want him, but the hiss between his teeth is not one of pain. It's of arousal, a pure unadulterated need that mirrors my own.

Pike tugs at my hair with one hand, pushing his pants down to his feet with the other, kicking them off.

And there he is. Naked before me. The sight causes me to gasp. Pike's body is a work of art, all chorded and lean muscle. His tattoos wrap around his hips in an intricate design I want to trace with my fingers and my tongue. His abs are outlined in shadows so deep they look as if they were drawn on. He's utter perfection. It's both infuriating and arousing that this man, out of all men, one who acts like the devil himself, is sculpted in the image of a god. An angel wearing a halo of hate and pain that penetrates my soul.

His cock is as enormous and intimidating as the rest of him. Jutting out before him, grazing his belly button, making me fearful, but in a very different way.

He strokes himself. Once, slowly, and I'm entranced by the movement, fighting the urge to reach out and grab it myself to find out what it would feel like in my own hand.

Pike slowly looks me over, and my body heats under his gaze. I'm nearly naked with my legs spread before him. Suddenly, I've never felt so exposed. I clasp my legs together, and he immediately releases his hold in my hair to pry them back apart. His eyes grow even darker as he fixates on the wetness pooling there. I didn't think it was possible, but he looks even hungrier than before.

His nostrils flare, and again, I find myself afraid of what he's capable of, but for an entirely different reason.

Pike covers me again with his body, tugging my breasts from the cups of my bra. He licks at one of my nipples then bites down. I groan at the sting of pleasure and arch my back, silently pleading for more. When his now naked shaft connects with my clit and throbs against me, I cry out. I cry out when my insides twist with need and unmet pleasure.

He licks and sucks my nipple, and I take a fistful of his hair, holding him against me, lifting my hips in a silent command for more.

He lifts his head and releases my nipple with a pop, the cool air meets the wetness and hardens them even more. He reaches between us and grabs the base of his shaft in his fist. His hand is large yet his cock still looks massive in his grip. He slides one hand behind my head, once again tangling it in my hair. His other moves to my lower back, raising my hips off the bed. He kisses me again, hard, furiously. There's a prodding at my entrance. Heated steel against silk. He groans into my mouth as he surges forward, impaling me with his massive cock that stretches me until I think I'm about to break. My eyes water, tears spill from the corners. It burns and hurts, and I never want it to stop.

He moves his lips to my eyes and licks away tears I didn't know had fallen. It hurts, so much, not just in my body, but in my heart.

"You're so fucking tight," he says on a strangled groan. "Fuck, you feel so good. So much better than anything…" he struggles to say, trailing off. "I thought about this. About you. So much. Fuck, Mic."

The way his face twists in agony and pleasure encourages me further. I lift my hips, taking him deeper, and still, it's not enough. The pain subsides with the movement, so I do it again.

He hisses, raising his eyes to the ceiling then pressing them shut.

I do it again.

His eyes open and meet mine. I give him a daring look that says *do your worst*. He smiles in reply, thrusting even harder, touching me even deeper.

And the battle resumes.

I meet him thrust for thrust as we hold each other's gaze.

He stills then pulls out and pushes forward with such force

my head hits the headboard, but I don't care. The sensation of having him inside of me, stretching me, filling me, is so great that I'm about to burst apart.

He holds me still in his arms, pulling me onto him while thrusting in fast hard strokes so that I feel all of him, everything he has to give. It's overwhelming, and yet it's perfect in the same way it's imperfect.

Like Pike.

"I fucking hate you," I groan against his lips, as he kisses me once more, but I don't mean it.

"I fucking hate you, too," he sneers, and I know he doesn't mean it either.

We should, but we don't. We can't.

How can I hate someone who is a part of me?

We're not enemies. We're victims of circumstance, caught up in what we think we should be doing while consumed by what we want to be doing to each other.

I raise my hips again, and his thrusting becomes wild and erratic until the tightness in my stomach explodes into a burst of feeling, shattering me to pieces like a sledgehammer to a window.

"Pike!" I cry out as the sensations overwhelm me in wave after wave of pleasure that has me seeing nothing but white.

Pike's cock hardens even more inside me. "Mic," he growls, and with a moan that has me coming even harder as I feel him come in long hot spurts, filling my body…while breaking my fucking heart. "Oh, fuck, Mic. What have we done?"

"I don't know," I reply, another tear spilling from my eye.

He licks the falling tear from my check. "This changes everything."

His words a vast contrast to what he said after our kiss on the curb.

I place my hand on his face. He turns his head and kissed my palm.

Pike and I aren't at war. We never were.

We are what's left over after the battle's already been lost on both sides.

We're not soldiers.

We're carnage.

CHAPTER TWENTY-SEVEN
PIKE

I KNOW WHAT I WANT, AND WHAT I WANT IS MICKEY. SHE'S NOT going to fight this battle alone. I'm going to fight it with her. I've spent all morning preparing plans to keep her safe while taking out the entire fucking Fourth Reich starting with Darius himself.

I'm standing at the register. The bell above the door chimes after a customer leaves. There's a sound in the back room. Laughter coming from Mickey and Thorne as they arrange antique candlesticks to take pictures for the website.

I never understood the importance of sound until today.

Sound is an incredible thing. The sound of Mickey's laughter. The sound of Thorne's nails tapping on keys. The camera clicking away. Even the ringing of the bell above the door of the shop. The sound of Mic moaning my name as I make her come. That one is a personal favorite.

It's the sound of normal. Maybe, not normal for others, but normal for us.

And I'm going to protect that new normal, at whatever fucking cost.

Another sound that has nothing to do with our new normal

comes from the parking lot outside, screeching tires on the asphalt.

Racing outside, I realize Mickey is close on my heels. "Stay back," I tell her as a flatbed truck skids to a halt in front of the shop.

I watch as familiar skeleton-clad men get out of the truck. They're carrying someone with a burlap hood covering his head. I recognize the burlap sack and the man underneath it immediately.

I go for my gun.

"Touch the gun, and he dies," one of them warns as they shove Gutter to his knees.

One of the armed men rips the hood from Gutter's head. He blinks away the blur. Then, his eyes land on me. He smiles. "It's not your fault, Pike. I had this comin' a long time, so don't go blaming yourself. It ain't your fault. I don't blame you. You're the best thing that's ever happened in my life. I consider you to be a son to me. Don't go getting yourself killed for a nobody like me either. You hear me?"

One man saunters over to him with a crowbar in hand. "No!" I shout, again reaching for my gun. Another one of the men fires at my feet in warning, creating a patchwork of holes in the asphalt.

"I love you, kid," Gutter says with a jerk of his chin.

It's only a second, but it feels like hours as the man rears back and bashes in the back of Gutter's skull.

Bullets or not, I race over to Gutter, firing my own gun at the truck that's now speeding away.

I drop the gun and pull Gutter into my arms, but there's no way he's alive. There's too much blood. I lift his head, and chunks of it fall to the parking lot. And not enough skull. I frantically try press the fragments of bone against the blood and gore oozing from his brain as if I can bring him back to life if I can just make his head whole again. "Gutter. Fuck, Gutter.

Don't be dead," I yell at him. "I didn't die on you, so you can't die on me," I say on a strangled sob. Dropping the piece of his skull to the asphalt, I tug his gaunt lifeless body against mine. "You can't fucking die on me!" I yell, but I know he can't hear me.

He'll never hear me again.

Mickey

"The sound of the tires on the pavement. It will always remind me of that moment. Of him," Pike says, sounding far away, as if he isn't in the same room as me. He's still covered in Gutter's blood.

I make a move to touch him, and he steps away.

"Echoic memory. Another name for sound memory. It registers specific moments and connects them to auditory information," I rattle on, realizing that a lesson in how sound memory works isn't really what Pike is looking for right now. I grimace, "Sorry."

He smiles, but it only makes him look sadder. "Don't ever apologize for being smart, Mic. It's your thing. Own that shit."

His gaze wanders around the bedroom like he's noticing it for the first time. He pads around the room, running his hands against the walls, looking truly lost.

He stills when he comes to a picture on the nightstand of him and Gutter holding up fish and grinning like idiots. He picks it up and runs his hands over the image.

My heart breaks for him as his eyes glass over. His shoulders slump in defeat. Slowly, he sets the picture back down. Straightening it several times. "How did you survive the death of your entire family?" he asks in a whisper that I wouldn't recognize as his voice if I hadn't seen the words pass through his lips with my own eyes.

Pike drops to the floor, and I join him, our backs to the bed. I

221

recognize the pain in his eyes. The questions. The blame. I feel it as if it's my own because in a way I own that kind of pain. I don't think before I act. Reaching out, I wrap my arm around his head and pull him down onto my lap.

"In some ways, I didn't," I confess, smoothing back his hair, petting him as if he were a stray cat in need of affection. "A big part of me died when they did, and what's left of me isn't someone I recognize anymore."

Pike leans into my touch. I clear my throat, choking back tears he doesn't need to see me shed right now. "You know," I offer, "One thing that helps is talking to them."

"I've heard you talking to them before," Pike replies. "You were talking to them when I first met you that night. Thought you were crazy."

"You weren't wrong. I was delirious that night, but even now, it's not something I try and hide. I don't care if people think I'm crazy. It helps me to imagine that they're all around me, here whenever I need them or when it all gets to be too much and I think I can't…" I sniffle. "You know, even in my own imagination, my sister Mallory still pesters me."

"I think I would have liked Mallory," he says softly.

I smile. "I think she would have liked you." I chuckle, imagining how Mallory's boy-crazy eyes would look the first time she saw Pike. "Too much."

"Does it ever stop hurting?" he asks, staring up at the ceiling.

"No," I reply honestly. "But the hurt changes over time. It morphs from something that feels like hands wrapped around your neck choking you to something that's like someone constantly pinching your skin. It still hurts, but it's a pain you learn to live with."

"Your revenge. You think getting it will make it hurt even less?" he asks.

"It might not make it hurt less, but I think it will make

living with it more bearable. In the end, it's not about my pain, but making them suffer for what they've done. Making them feel what they felt, what I feel."

Pike is quiet as I pet his head. "You know I can't stay," I say with a sigh. Tears form in my eyes. "Not because I don't want to, but because I have to go. I have to finish what I started."

He doesn't reply.

I look down to find his eyes closed.

For the moment, sleep makes him look peaceful. That is, until his hands twitch. Even in his sleep, Pike's hands are balled up into fists, his knuckles white and ready for a fight.

But this fight is mine. They started it. I'll be the one to end it.

And if everything goes the way it should, Pike won't be caught in the crossfire.

CHAPTER TWENTY-EIGHT
PIKE

I WAKE TO WHAT SOUNDS LIKE A THOUSAND CATS PATTERING ACROSS the roof. The room smells like fresh earth. It's raining, I realize as I blink off the blur of sleep.

Gutter is dead, and there's a piece of me missing. Not just in my heart, but in my bed. It's empty and cold.

I turn my head and find that Mickey is no longer asleep next to me. A quick scan of the room, and I find her standing at the window. She's bare-legged, wearing a large white sweater that hangs off one shoulder and is just long enough to cover her ass, revealing the smooth slope of her lean athletic thighs. The long sleeves cover her hands, the excess material gathered in her palms like makeshift gloves.

She's beautiful in a way that makes me realize I've never understood beauty before. My gut twists with the same need I felt last night as I watched her sleep. The need to keep her safe, to keep her happy.

To keep *her*.

It's stronger than any other compulsion I ever felt before, and it's because it's not a compulsion at all. It's just her.

For a moment, I watch her silently as she leans one shoulder against the window pane. Her eyes are focused upward on the sky, watching the storm as it passes. She raises her hand and pushes her sleeve to her wrist, pressing her fingertips to the glass as if she's trying to close the distance between her and the rain.

I realize she's aware that I'm awake when she speaks although she keeps her eyes focused out the window. "I once asked my father if he could see what I saw in the raindrops. The way the light shines differently off each one. The varying shapes, the different colors they reflect." Her voice is eerily calm and soft. "He told me no. He said that it takes a special gift like mine to be able to find something unique about each drop where most people just see water falling from the sky."

Sliding my feet off the side of the bed, I push to my feet and pad over to Mickey, leaning against the wall next to the window so I can face her, glancing momentarily at the rain that has her so fixated.

She flattens her palm to the glass. "It's…I think it's a shame that people can't see what I see, yet sometimes, I wish I could see it as they do."

I'm taken aback by the thought that she wants to be like everyone else because Mickey isn't like anyone else. Not even close. She's a different species of human, one I hate to admit, that I actually like, respect even. "It's a gift. It's *your* gift. Don't wish it away. It's what makes you…" I wave my hand at her, wishing I was as good with words as she is. "You."

She leans the side of her head against the window, shifting to face me. I'm met with bloodshot eyes and tear stained cheeks. Mickey's been crying. Noticing where my attention is focused, she wipes her cheek with the sleeve of her sweater.

"It's a curse in the same way that it's also a gift." Her eyes glass over as they fill with tears. Her calm voice grows shaky, catching in her throat. "There are billions of people on the earth, but none of them are like you, Pike. You're not just water falling from the sky. You're so unique and so special, and no one will ever see you the way I do. And because of this curse and this memory, I can't ever unsee you." She sniffles, yet it's me who feels my chest tightening and my throat closing. She blinks and a tear spills down her cheek, traveling the same path as the stains of tears that came before it. "Even if I wanted to. Even if I try really hard. You'll be here." She presses my hand to her temple. "Reflecting a different kind of light than anyone else."

"You don't ever have to unsee me," I tell her. "I'll be right here. With you."

I grab her wrist and press her palm against my chest so she can feel the beating of my heart. Her wet lashes flutter against her cheeks as she looks up at me with uncertainty in her eyes. I have no words of comfort to offer her. No words of encouragement or meaning. Nothing that can make her feel better because I have no idea what the future holds for either of us. I tug her into my chest and wrap my arms around her, resting my chin on the top of her head. She fits so perfectly against me, in this room, and in my life.

I lift her up and carry her back to bed, where I lay down with her on top of me, keeping her soft body pressed against mine as she sobs against my skin. Her tears spilling down the side of my chest in a warm stream of contagious poison that pricks at my eyes, threatening tears I never knew I was capable of producing.

She clutches at my chest, nails digging into my skin. I grit my teeth and take it because it's the least I can do after she comforted me last night. After a few moments, she stills. The crying stops, and the rhythm of her breathing evens out and slows. She's asleep.

My chest constricts, and it's not because of Mickey's weight. She's not heavy enough to bruise, never mind crush my chest.

With my lips pressed into Mickey's hair, I inhale the smell of her girly shampoo as her little exhales heat the skin at the crook of my neck. I watch over her head through the window as the rain comes down harder and harder. I squint and try to discern one raindrop from the next as it falls down in sheets, blurring the sky. Of course, I can't do what she can. It all looks like water to me.

You're not just water falling from the sky. You're so unique and so special and no one will ever see you the way I do.

No one has ever said anything like that to me and more, I never would have cared if anyone said that to me before. But I care now and only because of her.

I might not be able to see one rain drop from the next, but I don't need to tell the difference in the rain to feel a difference taking place in my heart. To be able to see special and unique in something others might otherwise look over as one of the masses.

She sees me, and I see her.

And right now, my own little rain drop is fast asleep on my chest. I can't offer her anything other than a warm body. A chest to cry on. It's all I have, and it's hers for the taking.

The tears that had threatened to spill make their presence known and flow past my lips into Mickey's hair. For her and her family and what they've gone through. For Gutter.

All I have to give her is me.

And I know it's not enough.

After a while, I place her beside me and dress to finish making my plans that got interrupted when Gutter was murdered on my fucking doorstep. I check in on Mickey a few times throughout the day, and each time, she's sleeping with new tear stains lining her cheeks and I can feel them as if her sadness and mine are one in the same.

When the day is over and the plans have been made, I trudge back to my apartment, ready to tell Mickey that I'm not going to risk her life and that I'll help her get her revenge as if it's my own, but this time, she isn't crying or sleeping.

Mickey's gone.

And so is my gun.

CHAPTER TWENTY-NINE
MICKEY

"I THOUGHT YOU LEFT ME THERE TO DIE," I SAY ANGRILY.

"I thought you were dead," Darius replies just as enraged.

The thing about Darius Alban is that when he says something or asks a question, he's always asking something else entirely. The trick is to read into the real meaning behind his words. It's something I've perfected over the years.

He smiles curiously. "We were waiting for Pike to come exact his revenge on us."

What did you tell him? Is what he is really asking.

"He doesn't know that it was you who stole his shipment," I lie. "Or that you are the one who returned it. He doesn't know I'm with you. I didn't tell him anything. I faked a brain injury."

"How did you manage to do that?" He raises a suspicious eyebrow and crosses one leg over the other.

I'm trying to figure out if you're lying.

I stretch the truth. "Pike knocked me out when the others ran off." I narrow my eyes at the men who came with me that night. "When I came to, I told him that I didn't remember why I was there or who I was with. I convinced him that I'd lost my memory."

"And he believed you?"

This is very clever. If it's actually true.

I nod. "He gave me a lie detector test. I passed."

"He didn't see the brand?" he asks, suspiciously.

Did he see you naked?

"No. Another woman was responsible for my care, and she never saw anything. If she did, she didn't know what it was and didn't say anything."

"Did he hurt you, my dear?" Darius asks, playing with the ends of his mustache.

Did he fuck you?

"Nothing I couldn't handle," I answer, with my chin up and my hands behind my back like a good soldier. "This didn't happen until I escaped." I motion to my leg.

"He did not rape you?" he asks as if he can't believe it because apparently I'm super rape-able.

This one he actually means.

I shake my head. "No. His interests were in finding out who I was working for. He spent his time with me trying to trigger my memory."

Darius seems satisfied with my answers to his inquisition. He slaps the arms of the chair and rises to his feet. His face plastered with a victorious smile. "Welcome home, Michaela." He opens his arms and wraps me into a hug. His heart beats against my cheek, and I resent each and every thump. "Our plans will continue as planned. You are a smart girl. I knew you would not let us down." He snaps his fingers. "Someone get Banjo in here, and have him take care of her wound."

The wound he's referring to is the self-inflicted gunshot to my thigh. It's gushing blood through the piece of Pike's t-shirt I'd wrapped around it.

If you're going to head back into hell and run back to the devil himself, you go prepared or not at all.

Darius places his arms around my shoulder and snaps his fingers in the air. One of his men opens the door behind his chair. "Only now, we have much to celebrate because your betrothed is finally home."

Slowly, a figure appears from the shadows until he's standing in front of the firelight. He's tall and muscular. His shirtless, pale torso covered with hateful racist tattoos that extend up the back of his bald head to the center of his scalp.

Darius lifts his arm from my shoulder. "Go on. Greet your fiancé."

I walk up to Percy and put on my best smile. I fake amazement in my eyes like I'm happy the fucking skinhead has been released from prison where he deserved to rot plus much worse. "Percy. Welcome home."

Percy grabs my wrist and lifts my hand to his disgusting thin lips. "So, we finally see each other again," he says, undressing me with his eyes. I try not to gag as he brushes his lips over my knuckles once again by imagining what his corpse will look like piled on top of his father's.

On that thought, I take a deep breath, and even with a gushing bullet wound pounding with pain in my thigh, I finally manage a real smile.

CHAPTER THIRTY
MICKEY

I HEAR A FAINT CRY. I SHAKE IT OFF AS THE WIND, BUT I HEAR IT again. It's not the wind. It's human. Female. And…*familiar.*

I leave the room and follow the sound until I'm in the warehouse in the back of the property. I push open the doors. It's pitch black, but the echoing cries tell me I'm in the right place.

I follow the sobs until I stop at what looks like a dog's cage.

Inside, curled in a ball, is an emaciated girl.

"What the fuck have they been doing since I've been gone?" I mutter.

The girl scrambles to the other side of the cage, making herself as small as possible.

"It's okay. I'm not going to hurt you," I tell her. "I'll get you out of here, I promise."

Her body turns to stone. I don't even see her back rising with her breaths. Then, ever so slowly, she raises her head, revealing sunken grey eyes the same color as mine.

I'm seeing things. I know I am. It's one of my imaginary conversations. It has to be. But why would I imagine this situation?

"Mickey?"

I take a step back. Never in my imagination has anyone

spoken before. Not Mallory or Maya or Mindy or my mother or even my father.

But, that's because this isn't my imagination. This is real. *She* is real.

I drop to the floor and grab the bars in both of my hands to steady myself. As a logical person, this isn't just illogical, and yet it isn't impossible.

It just can't be.

She can't be.

The girl crawls over to me and mirrors my position on her knees. I know for certain this moment is real when my sister places her hand over mine. I choke on a sob.

"Mindy?"

PREPPY PART ONE (Book 5)

PREPPY PART TWO (Book 6)

PREPPY PART THREE (Book 7)

Smoke & Frankie's Story (Standalone)

UP IN SMOKE (Spinoff)

Nine & Lenny's Story

NINE, THE TALE OF KEVIN CLEARWATER

King & Doe's Novella

King of the Causeway

Pike's Story (Duet)

Pike (Book 1)

Pawn (Book 2)

ABOUT THE AUTHOR

T.M. Frazier never imagined that a single person would ever read a word she wrote when she published her first book, The Dark Light of Day.

Now, she's a USA Today bestselling author several times over. Her books have been translated into numerous languages and published all around the world.

T.M. enjoys writing what she calls 'wrong side of the tracks' romance with sexy, morally corrupt anti-heroes and ballsy heroines.

Her books have been described as raw, dark and gritty. Basically, while some authors are great at describing a flower as it blooms, T.M. is better at describing it in the final stages of decay.

She loves meeting her readers, but if you see her at an event please don't pinch her because she's not ready to wake up from this amazing dream.

For more information please visit her website www.tmfrazierbooks.com

FACEBOOK: facebook.com/tmfrazierbooks

TWITTER: twitter.com/tm_frazier

INSTAGRAM: instagram.com/t.m.frazier

JOIN MY FACEBOOK GROUP, FRAZIERLAND: www.facebook.com/groups/tmfrazierland